W9-BII-694

DIABLO CREEK

DIABLO CREEK

TED SIMMONS

Tallahassee, Florida

Copyright © 2007 by Ted Simmons

Cover art copyright © 2007 by Mark Simmons

All rights reserved. No part of this book may be reproduced in any form or by any means, electronic or mechanical, including photocopying, recording, or by any information storage and retrieval system, without permission in writing from the publisher, except for brief quotations contained in critical articles and reviews.

Inquiries should be addressed to:
CyPress Publications
P.O. Box 2636
Tallahassee, Florida 32316-2636
http://cypress-starpublications.com
lraymond@nettally.com

Library of Congress Cataloging-in-Publication Data

Simmons, Ted, 1937–
  Diablo Creek / Ted Simmons. — 1st ed.
      p. cm.
  Summary: When sixteen-year-old Pete and his best friend Jerrod courageously face bullies and bullets while helping illegal immigrants from Nicaragua, enslaved by an important citizen of their town of Bennington, Texas, Pete is finally able to resolve some issues with his father, who died eight years earlier.
  ISBN-13: 978-0-9776958-7-4 (pbk.)
  ISBN-10: 0-9776958-7-5 (pbk.)
  [1. Illegal aliens—Fiction. 2. Drug traffic—Fiction. 3. High schools—Fiction. 4. Schools—Fiction. 5. Nicaraguans—United States—Fiction. 6. Murder—Fiction. 7. Single-parent families—Fiction. 8. Texas—Fiction.] I. Title.

PZ7.S59187Dia 2007
[Fic]—dc22

                              2007031043

ISBN 13: 978-0-9776958-7-4
ISBN 10: 0-9776958-7-5

First Edition

Dedication

For Brianna, Taylor, Mandy and Conner.
They haven't yet invented a word to
describe my pride in you.

CHAPTER 1

Jerrod and I were on this piddly piece of a gravel road, surrounded by swirling muddy water. We'd just managed to wade through this bitchin', waist-high torrent that'd cut through the roadway and temporarily stranded us. I'm not the bravest guy in the world, far from it, but sometimes you gotta do what you gotta do. As the adrenaline drained away, my breathing slowed and I started to relax. Then I caught this flash of blue and white in the sea of brown.

The current had pushed a tangled pile of trash up against the submerged roadbed we'd just forded. It was made up of these jagged tree limbs and pieces of boards sticking up every which way, with smaller branches and dead brush holding the whole mess together. I shielded my eyes from the morning sun so I could see what looked like clothing mixed in with the trash. Probably just some laundry washed off some poor bozo's clothesline a hundred miles upriver.

Jerrod waded back into the water.

"What the heck you doing?" I yelled. "Why are you going back?"

"Just a ways," he said. "I wanta see what that is."

"Are you nuts?"

"Could be. But I'm curious."

"What is it?"

1

"Don't know. Shut up and let me look."

By now, part of the trash pile had pushed right up onto the road. Jerrod kept slip-slipping his way toward it with me on his tail. Every time he stopped to shift his weight to the other foot, I bumped into his rear end.

"I know we're friends," he said, "but not that good." He reached back, grabbed my arm and pulled me around beside him. "Is that what I think it is?"

I tried to answer, but couldn't. It felt like a tennis ball had lodged in my throat.

There was no doubt about what we were seeing. The blue and white were a pair of jeans and a dirty, torn tee-shirt. What really got me, though, was what I could see between the jeans and the shirt—a glistening strip of brown skin. And one of the limbs I'd thought was part of a tree was actually a human arm. A real human arm, twisted around a two-by-four, jutting out of the pile at a crazy angle.

CHAPTER 2

When I'd dragged myself out of bed that morning, I had zero idea things would turn so dramatic. Hell, I'd planned the laziest Saturday I could get away with. How could I know I'd manage to escape death, find a body, and seriously jeopardize my mother's trust? And that I'd accomplish this amazing feat before noon.

I was sleepily dipping my spoon in the bowl and watching my Cheerios rearrange themselves when I heard scratching at the door. *Our stupid dog's in the house, isn't she? Anyways, who cares?* I couldn't see what was making the noise without actually dragging my body out of the chair, so I tried to ignore it. It wasn't about to be ignored, though, so I jumped up and threw the door open. My friend Jerrod was on all fours with his face twisted up at me in a goofy hound-dog parody. His tongue was hanging out. Actually, Goofy would've been embarrassed.

"Woof," he said, making it sound like a question.

I slammed the door in his face and went back to contemplating my cereal. Jerrod walked in, turned a chair backwards, and sat. He reached into the box for a handful of Cheerios.

"Y'all alone?" he drawled.

I didn't answer for a minute, then said, "Not now, I'm not."

"Finish up. We got places to go."

"Bug off."

"Things to do. Sights to see."

In my bedroom, Jerrod lay on the floor with his head resting on my crumpled bedspread. I tried to pull it away so I could make the bed, but he ignored me. I had big plans to spend the morning imitating a vegetable, but Jerrod was on a mission and wouldn't be interrupted.

"Jeez, Pete, don't wimp out on me. What's the big deal?"

Jerrod buzzes through life like he's surrounded by some kinda force field protecting him from everything bad. If something breaks through anyway and dumps him on his butt, he gets up, shrugs his chunky shoulders, and smashes on ahead. I, on the other hand, agonize over things that haven't happened yet and probably never will.

I said, "That guy we read about in the paper yesterday."

"*You* read about in the paper. You know I never touch the nasty things. Besides, what guy?"

"Yeah, but we talked about it. The one who drowned. He was nineteen. Maybe if he'd wimped out on his friends, he'd still be alive."

"The idiot went wading in shallow water, fell into a hole he couldn't see, cracked his head."

"And your point?"

"We're not gonna go wading. We'll stand on dry land and just look. C'mon, ol' buddy, lighten up. What trouble can we get into?"

I had to admit what Jerrod had in mind didn't sound danger-ous. He's about the only real friend I've made in the year and a half I've lived in this podunk town of Bennington, Texas, so it was pretty easy to convince me to do what I wanted to anyway—sort of like persuading a dog he ought to quit hanging back and dig into his kibble.

"Okay," I said, "but we've gotta go somewhere where there's not a lot of people. I don't want someone seeing me and blabbing to Mom."

"Excellent, my man."

I rode my bike slowly to Jerrod's place, so he could keep up, jogging alongside. He wasn't in all that bad shape, considering he was continually feeding his face and never played any sports or did any work he didn't have to. I'm a lot taller than him, skinnier, too, and not too great at most sports, but I can run circles around Jerrod on the track.

He went behind his house to the big yellow shed standing sentinel at the end of the garden. He grabbed his own bike, brushing aside a haphazard collection of garden tools stacked against it. Even though it was a beaut, an almost-new, olive-green mountain bike, Jerrod rarely rode it. He said he was getting too old for transportation that didn't involve a minimum of six gasoline-powered cylinders.

"For cryin' out loud, how can you treat your bike like that?" I asked. "Look at it, the fenders are dented already."

"It looks better than yours, scuzz-ball."

Sometimes Jerrod really hacks me off. I said, "I've had mine for five years, not five minutes. Besides, it looked this way when I got it. In fact, it looks a helluva lot *better* today than when I got it."

"We've all got our priorities, and this bike isn't mine. I'm gonna get me a car soon anyways."

I decided I'd better shut up. I figured I'd be nursing along my old bike till I'm thirty, while here he was trading in a brand new one on a car. I sure-as-hell didn't want Jerrod to think I was jealous of him, because I wasn't. Much.

Jerrod ran into the house to get a couple of candy bars. He insisted we have "a little trail-grub for our adventure." Unlike me, Jerrod Wilson has a father as well as a mother, but they both work Saturdays, so no one was home. Besides, they almost never tell Jerrod where he can go or where he can't. Given the chance, I'd take Jerrod's life in a millisecond. Of course, in two milliseconds I'd feel guilty as hell, thinking of my mom sitting alone in an empty house. I hate it when I feel that way. Guilt. The Grayson curse.

We rode up to the north side of town, where houses come in bright colors—sky blue, sea blue, faded shrimp, white with pink trim like crab meat. They were crowded together so one yard's rusted car on blocks butted into the next yard's carefully tended roses. I always thought my house was little, compared to Jerrod's palatial digs, but next to these places it was huge. From kitchen windows I could smell the foods of the south and the southwest all jumbled together. Corn meal and chilies. Fried chickens and potatoes. These were combinations I'd come to associate with the state I now called home.

Little kids were everywhere, dancing around in the morning sunshine, some of them only half-dressed, shining bronze-colored bodies chasing soccer balls in the streets. They shouted at each other in Spanish.

"You understanding them?" asked Jerrod.

"Almost nothing."

"After two years of Spanish? Whoo-whee! The State of Texas is definitely wasting their tax dollars on Peter Grayson."

"They're not exactly using words outta my textbooks, you idiot. *Tu idiota.*"

I began to worry maybe it wasn't such a hot idea to be up here. It wouldn't have taken many neural connections in some of the older guys' brains to recognize Jerrod and I were from Southside. Getting the crap beat out of me wasn't my concept of an ideal morning. *Jeez, Grayson, what a wuss.* I hate it when I worry like that.

Luckily, nobody paid us any attention, so we relaxed and looked for the river. We could see silvery patches of water through the trees behind the houses. When we reached a place where the buildings and the pavement both ended, a narrow gravel road cut to the right and went over a little rise. At the top, we stopped and stared. The road was the only piece of dry land visible, a thin gray line extending out into a sea of brown water. Awesome.

"C'mon, peckerhead," said Jerrod, as he tore off like a terrier who'd just tunneled under the fence.

"Wait. We shouldn't . . ."

But Jerrod was already gone, pedaling like crazy.

Damn. I yelled, "Wait up, man."

Without turning, he waved for me to catch up. I rode hard, my knees pumping high, trying to force some speed out of the bike I'd outgrown years before.

We both slowed when I reached him, and we rode together in silence. The narrow gravel road stretched ahead like a gray ribbon floating on chocolate milk.

I looked to the left for some sign of Diablo Creek, the stream that meandered through these fields before merging with the Brazos River ahead. Diablo Creek had disappeared! It hadn't dried up in the brutal Texas heat, just the opposite. It was hidden beneath a plain of ugly, brown water. Usually, herds of cows would be happily munching away at the grass on the banks of the creek. Now there were no cows, no grass, no creek. Just miles of dirty water.

The road took a sharp right and ran parallel to cottonwood trees I was pretty sure marked the edge of where the Brazos River ought to be. You could only see the top half of the trees. On both sides of the trees, the plain of still water gave way to movement, I mean really powerful movement. According to the morning news, the river was running thirty-five feet above normal in our area and expected to crest even higher as more water flooded in from the North Texas watershed.

Ahead, the road dipped, brown current washing over it.

"Far enough, Jerrod. Let's turn back."

"Jeez, Pete, don't be such a jerk-off. We can go a little further." He shook his head. "We'll barely get our friggin' tires wet."

We passed a mess of broken trees and pieces of wood piled up between us and the river. Behind them, the water churned, moving in strange patterns, like swirls and spirals tattooed on a biker's arms. Soon the pathway disappeared completely. For us, this was the end of the road.

We stopped to watch the river rushing past. I said, "My Uncle Tyler told me about a flood he'd watched once. He saw a dead cow all bloated up and floating with its left legs in the water and its right legs sticking up into the air."

"Gross."

"If you fell into this, do you suppose any of your body parts would stick up as your corpse headed south?"

When we turned back, I said to Jerrod, "Doesn't that pile of stuff look like it's moved closer?"

"What stuff."

"That one, in front of us, dumbo. All that wood and junk. It's pushed right up onto the road."

"You're imagining things."

"No way. Look, the water's trying to get around it."

"I don't see what . . ."

"The gravel. It's washing away. Oh, man."

I glanced over at Jerrod, and then I really started to panic. I'd never seen him look so scared. Never seen him scared at all. I turned back to stare at the swirling water now surging across the roadway and blocking our retreat. My legs started to shake, my chest got tight, and I felt like I might pee my pants.

We were trapped on a shrinking island in the middle of a sea of angry water.

We were trapped, alone, and not a soul on earth knew where the hell we were.

CHAPTER 3

Jerrod's voice quavered. "Oh, man. Oh . . . man. What're we gonna do, Pete? What'll we do?" Even though he was speaking barely above a whisper, over the eerie silence of the floodwaters his voice sounded like metal scraping on metal. Instead of giving orders, taking control, Jerrod was asking me what to do. Me! I couldn't believe it. He wanted me to take charge, make some kind of decision, but it was all I could do to keep from embarrassing myself.

I closed my eyes for a second and took a couple of deep breaths, laid down my bike, and went over to where the water swirled over the roadway. I turned away so Jerrod wouldn't see I was as scared as he was. I hate when anybody sees how scared I am.

"I don't know what we're gonna do, Jerrod. But whatever it is, we sure-as-hell better do it quick. The water's gonna cut right through this gravel before you know it."

Frightened as I was, my mind was starting to work. Maybe underneath the surface, the water had already cut a ditch, and we'd fall into it like that guy who'd drowned the day before. I had visions of my body being sucked out into the current and bobbing around with all of the trash and dead livestock on the way to the Gulf.

"I'm going to walk my bike through the water, real slow," I told Jerrod. "If my front wheel drops into a hole, I can pull back. You

9

walk behind and be ready to grab me if I start to fall in. But be careful. No sense both of us drowning."

I swelled up a bit, proud of how selfless and mature I sounded, telling Jerrod to save himself if he couldn't save me. Nothing like a little touch of ego to give a person courage.

I gripped my handlebars tightly and started to walk, pushing the bike out in front of me as far as I could. I had one part of my mind on the swirling, ominous water, now almost up to the axle, and one part on tomorrow's headlines. *Local boy drowns. Body of sixteen-year-old Peter Grayson still missing.*

Little by little, we pushed our way through. At one point, just opposite the pile of trash, the wheel dipped down suddenly and another cold wave of fear passed through me. I jerked back. I tried it again, slowly, and found the hole kept going down and down into the murky water. I moved ahead, turtle slow. It seemed like it was just possible to push through it, but it was getting worse every second. We had to keep moving.

At the deepest point, the water pushed hard against my legs. Finally, I was up to my waist. All kindsa junk carried along by the torrent kept pounding the side of my legs. Worse, I could feel the gravel moving under my feet, like standing in shallow water at the beach as it rushes back out to sea for the next wave—that creepy feeling of sand washing away underfoot, making you dizzy and barely able to stay upright. I hate that feeling. It was hard to believe this had been a dry road just minutes before.

Finally, the struggle seemed to be paying off. We fought through the deepest part and up into shallower water. After what seemed like hours, we were on solid ground. I was so weak-kneed by then, all I could do was drop my bike and sit, only little-by-little aware of the jagged bits of Texas gravel poking into my body. My clothes were soaked to above the waist, and I was trying to figure out some story to tell my mom. Jerrod sprawled next to me, staring back at the stream of water cutting away at the path we'd just come through.

It was then we saw the blue jeans and the white tee-shirt and the skinny brown body tangled in the trash pile. I managed to get control of myself and edged forward with Jerrod. Sticking out of the tattered shirt was this shock of dark, nearly black hair. I crouched down to get a better view and saw a face, a boy's face. He and the tree limbs were wrapped around each other like a tangle of snakes viewed in freeze-frame. The guy was sure-as-hell dead, like *we'd* be if we didn't get out of there.

I started to back away, then stopped. *What if he's not dead?* We couldn't just leave him there without knowing. I pushed forward again. The water was battering the side of my legs, but I ignored it as I reached out to touch the kid's arm. It was cold, but that didn't mean anything, being in the water like that. I squeezed his hand and thought maybe I felt it squeeze back, just a bit.

"I think he's alive, Jerrod. He's still alive. We gotta do something."

Jerrod was already pulling away some of the brush the boy was tangled up in. As I grabbed a piece of weathered board, it started to move. The board, the boy, the entire pile of refuse was slipping sideways across the road.

"Oh, man. We gotta hurry or he's gone."

The two of us started to rip and tear away pieces of bushes, branches, bits of soggy cardboard, and what looked like old electrical wiring. Jerrod slipped and fell into the water with a huge splash. His head went under briefly, and he flailed his arms wildly. I caught a wrist and held him until he regained his footing. Jerrod's face was as white as cold ashes. His bravery had evaporated the minute his head went underwater. I didn't give him time to think about it, though, and went back to what we were doing.

Attacking the pile again, we worked even more feverishly, because the damn thing was picking up speed. We were finally able to each grab an arm and haul the boy backwards, free of the junk pile. Just in time, too, because with a big sucking sound, it rolled off the roadbed and broke into a dozen pieces that bobbed away in the muddy water.

We pulled the kid onto dry ground and laid him on his back. They'd given us a lesson in CPR at school, but I wasn't sure I could do it for real. Luckily, I could see he was already breathing. His chest was moving. He was alive.

He was barely conscious, though. I don't know how he'd been able to hang on and keep his head above water. I guess he managed because people can be capable of amazing things when they have to be. Apparently, this guy wasn't ready to die just yet.

Dark brown skin, kind of long, black hair plastered over his forehead. He looked Hispanic. He was one of the skinniest kids I'd ever seen. I thought he must be really young until I noticed a fuzz of black hair on his upper lip and his chin.

He was bruised and cut up pretty badly, all over his face and arms and on the strip of stomach that showed above his jeans. Not much blood though, so the cuts probably weren't deep, just scrapes, and the cold water kept them from bleeding too badly. On the right side of his forehead was this long, jagged scar that was completely healed and looked old. His whole face was puffed up and his lips were cracked like hard candy.

I bent down to listen as he opened and closed his mouth, kinda like a fish. Nothing came out but this gurgling sound. Then he started to cough. When he did, his eyes popped open and he stared at us, scared, like we were about to run him through with swords. He rolled to the side and put one arm over his head while his skinny body curled up like a spider splashed with hot water. He coughed and coughed, repeated painful spasms.

When his body quit shaking, he turned back over and sat up. We could see he was weak, and Jerrod grabbed his arm just as he was about to topple back over.

"What's your name?" I asked.

He didn't say anything, but stared ahead with eyes that seemed to be focused on China. Then he lowered his chin to his chest and mumbled, "Pedro."

"Pedro! Hey, we got the same name. I'm Peter, English for Pedro." Pedro smiled the tiniest bit.

"Where are you from?" He might've been floating down the Brazos for miles and miles. He didn't answer, but shook his head and looked down at his muddy jeans again. Maybe he doesn't speak much English.

"¿De dónde tu?. . ." My spoken Spanish was a bit lame, but Pedro looked up, and I could tell he understood what I was asking. Still, he shook his head and dropped his chin again. Wherever he'd come from, he wasn't telling.

"I'm in deep doodoo, Jerrod. Mom'll have a cow when she finds out where I've been. But there's not much I can do about it. We've gotta get Pedro to a doctor and call the police. Someone has to help him find his parents."

'No," Pedro yelled. *"No policía. No puedo volver. No puedo. Por favor.* Please. Please." He was shaking his head wildly, terrified.

"What's he saying?" asked Jerrod.

"I'm not sure. Something about he can't turn. Turn . . . turn. Maybe *return* . . . I think he's trying to tell us he can't go back. Wherever he came from, he can't go back."

I looked at Jerrod, and he raised his eyebrows and shrugged. He had no more idea of what to do than I did.

"Let's get back to your house, Jerrod, and dry off. We'll figure something out."

It was a long hike to the Wilsons' but we had no other choice. Pedro was too weak to ride on our handlebars. In fact, he was too weak to walk. We put him on the seat of my bike and took turns walking alongside, pushing him. He crossed his arms on the handlebars, laying his head on top of them. We must've made quite a picture, trudging back through Northside. The spiky-haired little kids stopped their play to stare, but kept their distance. We were just too weird.

An old brown car came around the corner and sputtered to a stop in one of the driveways. One of the little kids broke away from the crowd and ran to the car shouting, "Papa!" He hurled himself through the air to be caught by the man who'd stepped out of the car and turned with outstretched arms just in time for the catch. As we continued our journey, I tried to hold the image of that little boy and his father in my mind, but it kept slipping away, morphing into this other picture. The sky became a deeper blue and the trees were brilliant with New England reds and oranges and yellows. The car was white, shining and new. The smiling man who stood beside it wore a blue dress shirt and red tie and carried a briefcase. As I ran toward him, he dropped the briefcase and tossed his jacket back into the car. I dipped and then flew, shouting like Tarzan in the trees, hurtling toward the arms stretched out to catch me.

The moving picture slowed. I hung in mid-air as the image changed again. The man pressed back against the car and his smile faded. As I crashed into him, his arms dropped and my own arms slipped down his sides as I tried to cling to him. Tarzan's yell turned to a strangled cry.

"What's wrong, Pete?"

It took me a while to realize Jerrod was talking.

"What?"

"You made this crazy sound. You looked like you were somewhere else."

"It's nothing."

"Where were you?"

"I said forget it. I was here, all right?"

"Okay, okay."

I tried to get back to the problems at hand. What were we going to do about Pedro? What was I gonna do about disobeying Mom? Usually, I can think of a dozen answers to any problem and juggle 'em around, trying to choose the best one. But this problem with

Pedro and my mom had me beat. For once in my life, I couldn't figure out a single thing to do. It didn't help that an eight-year-old memory had thrust a shriveled hand out of the coffin I'd thought was safely, finally buried.

CHAPTER 4

Dad,

I suppose you (or anyone, really) would think it's funny my writing to you after all these years. Don't think it's because I still don't hurt, cause I do—a lot. There isn't a night goes by when I don't lay there in bed thinking what I could've done. If only—

They say, "if only" are the saddest two words in the English language. My friend Jerrod—you don't know about Jerrod, do you?—Jerrod says they're not the saddest words, just the stupidest. Seems he never worries about anything.

Anyway, don't ask me why I'm writing to someone who can't write me back, and who decided he didn't have time for me even when we lived in the same house. It's just there's so much shit going down right now, I've got to get it off my chest, somehow, and I sure as hell can't tell Mom about it. (I guess you're a little shocked by those bits of profanity I used just then. I'm not eight years old any more, in case you've lost track of time. Things have changed.)

Jerrod and I found this Spanish-speaking guy in the river, almost drowned. We hauled him off to Jerrod's tool shed till we could figure out what to do. I couldn't let Mom know about him because I wasn't supposed to be where I was when we found him. But that's another story. More later . . . .

Your son (just a reminder), Pete

CHAPTER 5

Inside the Wilsons' garden shed it was already hotter'n raisin toast. Before we moved to Texas, my mom and I had lived in Connecticut where the weather starts to turn cooler in September. Here it was still as hot as the Tex-Mex food I was trying to learn how to enjoy.

Jerrod brought out some towels and clothes for us to change into while our wet things dried. He stripped off and started to dry himself like he didn't have a care in the world. I couldn't help feeling self-conscious. I wanted to turn away from Jerrod and Pedro while I changed, but didn't. It was embarrassing enough just being embarrassed. I hate it when I'm embarrassed and know I shouldn't be.

Pedro hurt so badly, he couldn't manage to undress.

"Here," Jerrod said. "Let me help you get that shirt off. Grab that side, Pete, and peel it up real slow."

The jeans were a bigger problem. Pedro was too weak to support himself when we tried to pull them off.

"You're going to have to hold onto him, Pete, while I pull on his pants legs."

I held Pedro from behind while Jerrod tugged. Because the jeans were wet, it was like pulling the casing off a sausage. I could feel Pedro's ribs under my hands, and for a minute I was afraid they might break. I could barely stand to look at his naked body. He was unbelievably skinny, and his brown skin was mottled with these huge purple and yellow bruises. His ribs stuck out, making his chest look like an old washboard dirt road in the country. He reminded me of those pictures of starving kids in Africa.

I was relieved when we got Pedro and myself covered with some of Jerrod's old pants and shirts. Jerrod's clothes were too short and too wide for me, but Pedro was almost swallowed up in them. He disappeared into the fabric, except for his face and mop of black hair. He smiled for a second, just a flicker that came and was gone.

"Where were you born?" I asked Pedro, *en español.* I was sure my Spanish grammar was crappy, but I'd worked hard at vocabulary, so I knew a lot of words.

"Nicaragua, in the small village of Posoltega." Wow. Not only did he understand me, but I could understand him. Translating for Jerrod, I tried not to look too proud. I tried to make it seem like being a bilingual interpreter was something I did all the time.

"How did you come to the United States? To Texas?"

Pedro shook his head and stared at the floor. I tried another approach. "Did you come with your parents? Where can we find them?"

His eyes flashed at me, angry. But almost immediately they softened, and he looked to some far off place only he could see. Tears rolled down his cheeks, and he didn't try to wipe them away.

"*Muerto.* Dead. My father and my mother are dead. Except for Juan and Carlina and me, my whole family, all dead."

"What . . . how . . . ?"

"First came the rains. For many days, it would not stop. Never before had we seen rain like that."

Pedro closed his eyes, breathed in sharply, then let it out slowly. When he began to speak again, he struggled to find the words to describe the horror of the final hours of his village. Posoltega was on the banks of a small stream that often flooded. Every few years,

Pedro would help his family move their most valuable posses-
sions to a space under the roof where they'd be safe till the waters
receded.

"But this time it was different. This time it was the mud."

Pedro, his brother Juan, and sister Carlina were in the hills
gathering firewood during a break in the rains. They heard a sound
"like many trains" from up the valley and watched, unbelieving,
as a wall of mud, carrying boulders and trees, swept toward their
village.

"We could see people running, but they could not run fast
enough. One by one, they disappeared."

The wall of mud filled the valley from side to side. There was
no escape. Houses were flattened and submerged within seconds,
or thrown upward where shattered walls and roofs bounced on the
mud flow "like toys." When Pedro, Juan, and Carlina returned to
their home, there was no trace of it. The only evidence of where
it had been was a ragged, broken trunk of the flame tree that had
shaded the porch where their father liked to sit after a day in the
fields. A few red flowers clung to the very top. I could picture it
looking like a tattered flag, trying to fly bravely above all the deso-
lation.

"And your parents?"

Pedro shrugged. Finally, he said, "My father's body has never
been found. My mother was in a field, covered with rocks and
pieces of broken trees. You could see only her legs. The rest of her
was under the mud."

I couldn't help thinking how strange it was; if we hadn't found
Pedro, he'd have died the same way his parents did, only he had
to come all the way to the States to do it.

"How did you come here?" I asked Pedro. He looked away
quickly, saying nothing.

"All right, Einstein," Jerrod interrupted. "We're here. We're
dry. Now what?"

I got up and started pacing around the shed, talking partly to Jerrod but mostly to myself. I was cataloguing facts, organizing what we knew and didn't know about Pedro. I do that a lot. Cataloguing and organizing. Someone said I was "anal retentive," which sounds dirty but isn't.

"He won't tell us how he got here and where he's been staying. He got pretty spooked when I talked about doctors and police. It's my guess he's not exactly in this country legally."

"Well, duh," said Jerrod.

Off to the side, I could see Pedro straining to understand what I was saying. At my mention of "doctors" and "police," which sound almost the same in Spanish, he became visibly upset again. He lifted his hands in front of himself and waved them frantically, palms forward, as if he was fending off a blow. I shook my head, trying to reassure him.

"Okay, let's try to figure this out," I said, continuing my analysis of the facts. "Nicaragua's in Central America, way south of Mexico. So how'd he get here?"

We discussed all of the possibilities we could think of, but none of them made sense. He was a poor kid who'd lost everything but the clothes he was wearing. There was no way he could afford to pay for the long trip north.

"There's something he's not telling us, and it's bad."

"Something worse than watching your parents get buried in mud?"

I glanced again at Pedro, who was trying unsuccessfully to follow our conversation. His tear-stained face, the slump of his shoulders, everything about him warned me there *might* be almost worse things, terrible things he could not, or would not, discuss.

CHAPTER 6

I took Jerrod aside and said, "What we need to think about is what we're gonna do now."

"If we tell my dad, he'll tell the po . . . he'll advise the authorities, and they'll take it from there."

"Jeez, man. Is that what you wanta do? Get him sent back to a village that doesn't exist?"

"No." Jerrod shook his head. "No, I don't. But what's our choice? If he's an illegal alien, we can't march him down to Burger King to get a job. And we can't keep him a secret, can we?"

I thought for a minute. "Not forever. But long enough for him to get his strength back. When he's better, he can decide what he does next."

"You mean let him stay here?"

"Why not? How often do your parents use this shed?"

"My mother never does. My dad almost never. I do most of the yard work, except for a crew that comes every week or so to mow the lawn. And edge. And weed the flower beds."

I started to laugh, grateful for an excuse to break the tension. "What else is there? It must be an exhausting job, nipping the dead flowers off the chrysanthemums."

Jerrod stared at me like I'd gone crazy. Then he grinned and said, "It takes great patience and skill. You wouldn't want me to over-nip now, would you?"

21

We both laughed until I saw the newly stricken look on Pedro's face and felt a flood of guilt. There was no way Pedro could understand how Jerrod and I sometimes joked when things were getting a bit tense.

Jerrod pulled out an old twin-sized mattress from the back of a storage closet, some sheets, and blankets. I made up a bed for Pedro in the shed while Jerrod went to the kitchen to fix sandwiches, which he brought back with chips and a can of root beer.

As we watched Pedro wolf down the food, Jerrod looked around and said, "If this isn't a regular Motel 6." Then he smacked the side of his head and said, "Uh-oh."

"What?"

Jerrod dragged me outside. "Now he's eating, it's going to be just a matter of time before he has to . . . you know, take a dump. If we're keeping him a secret, he can't exactly walk up to the house and ask my mother to use the john."

"Not a problem," I said. "Although you, Mr. Wilson, are a renowned expert on anything having to do with food and the entire alimentary canal, including the process of elimination, it is I, Peter the Grayson, who will handle this." In my best fake-Texas accent, I added, "Guar-an-teed." I can do Texan real well, I think.

I dug a hole behind the shed and laid two boards over each side to form a makeshift privy. I told Pedro to only use it after dark, and we gave him this humongous coffee can to use during daytime emergencies. He caught on to what we were up to immediately—either that or my Spanish had *really* improved.

My jeans were dry, so I changed and headed for home after promising Pedro I'd bring him back some Spanish language books in the morning. He'd be bored out of his gourd in no time, if we didn't find some things for him to do. The books I had were children's books, easy readers I'd picked up during *Spanish I* my freshman year. They weren't exactly Gabriel Garcia Marquez, but I guessed a kid from a rural village in Nicaragua might not be into literary classics anyway. As opposed to a guy from Connecticut.

When I got home, my mom was just getting back from her job as a receptionist in a dentist's office. The position had been arranged before we even came to Texas, thanks to an old college friend of Mom's. She worked in the same office and had been trying to get us to move south since right after my dad died.

I remember overhearing Mom talking to her on the phone once. Mom was saying, ". . . of course the house has memories. But some of them are good ones, Sarah. Anyway, what can I do? He's lost his father. I can't very well tear him away from his friends, too."

I wanted to scream at her that no one, not my friends, not her, not anyone, could take away the pain I was feeling. No one could make me want to get out of the friggin' bed in the morning and face myself in the bathroom mirror. We could stay in Connecticut, move to Texas, move to Timbuktu, for God's sake. It wouldn't matter, because wherever we went, I could never escape from myself. I didn't say a word, though—just shut myself in my room.

Each weekday I went to school, did my homework, even got good grades. For almost eight years I was alive, but not fully living.

Now, in Texas at last, I was feeling, well . . . all right. Not great, but better. Who knows, Mom's friend Sarah might've been right all along. Maybe getting away from Connecticut years ago could have helped. Maybe not, though. Probably what it took was time.

Mom had stopped at the store after work, and I helped her put away the groceries. She had brought home a box of soda crackers even though we had an almost-full one in the cupboard. I hid the old one so I could bring it to Pedro.

"What did you do today?" she asked.

I kept my head in the food cupboard, rearranging things. "Nothing."

"Nothing?"

"Rode over to Jerrod's."

"On your bike? Doesn't he live across the highway in Oakview Terrace?"

"Yes, Mom. On my bike. I was careful, okay? I'm always care-ful, okay?" *Sixteen and she worries about where I ride my friggin' bike.*

She was quiet for a few minutes, taking groceries out of the sacks and placing them on the kitchen counter. "I thought I saw him coming here just as I was leaving for work."

"Yeah, he did. But then we went to his house. He came here, then we went there. Here. There. All right?"

I realized I was getting pretty snippy. *Watch it, Peter.* I caught my mother's eye and tried on a sappy smile.

"He had some . . . new books he wanted me to see."

"I thought you said Jerrod wasn't much of a bookworm."

"He's not. But his parents gave him a bunch of books, and he thought I'd be interested, being as I am one . . . a bookworm, I mean."

"That's nice."

"Uh, Mom?"

"Hmm?"

"When does Mrs. Sanchez clean the house again?"

"Tuesday. Why?"

"No reason. Just wondered."

As I left the kitchen, I glanced back and saw Mom was giving me that *What are you up to, now?* look—the one where she cocks her head to one side and halfway squints one eye. My question about Mrs. Sanchez? Or maybe she'd just realized I'd ridden my bike to Jerrod's house even though Jerrod had been on foot. My mind was racing to explain that away, and then I remembered something about telling lies—one lie can make you have to tell another one, and then another, till it's all a complicated mess. I ran for my room and got very busy on an English essay, even though it was Saturday night.

CHAPTER 7

What the heck we gonna do, Pete?"

Jerrod was whispering, a loud, dramatic stage-whisper. The only reason none of the other students paid any attention was they were way too busy with getting to their next classes on time. The hallway was filled with the noise of locker doors clanging, hurrying feet, appointments being made and unmade by voices shouting at each other in passing. Jerrod and I were pressed up against a wall, trying to avoid the mess.

"How hot?" I asked.

"They say close to a hundred. Summer's back. Pete, we've gotta do something. He'll roast in there."

"I know, I know. Maybe he'll leave if it gets too hot."

Jerrod shook his head. "I don't think so. When I looked in on him this morning, he was so sore he could barely move. I think he'll just lay there and die of heat stroke."

"You're probably right. Besides, he seems, like, terrified about being seen in public. Damn."

"So what happens now?" asked Jerrod.

"We should've thought of this yesterday when it started to heat up."

The shed *had* been hot Sunday afternoon, but tolerable. Since this was my first September in Texas, I didn't realize the break in the hot weather was just that—a break. I didn't know summer had only been taking a breather before another month or so of killer heat.

Sunday had been darn near comical. Jerrod and I had spent the entire day working out elaborate ways of getting into and out of the shed without his family noticing. I'd putter around in the back yard while Jerrod would busy himself in the kitchen. As soon as he was sure his parents were busy in the front half of the house, he'd rush out to grab me, and we'd dash into the shed with Pedro.

Getting out of the shed was another matter, since we couldn't be sure who might be looking out the kitchen window. We decided to use this old soccer ball as a prop. We'd leave the shed with the ball and kick it around a bit before Jerrod would break off and head for the kitchen to see if we'd been seen. Of course, neither Jerrod nor I had ever shown the slightest interest in soccer, and even if we had, we'd have been the last guys to actually get out and sweat in the afternoon sun. I was just cocky enough to think I could come up with an explanation if somebody pointed out that embarrassing fact.

Jerrod's sister Eileen was our biggest worry. Her bedroom was at the rear of the house. Every weekend she slept half the day, re-cuperating from some hot date the night before. She was a senior at Bennington High, just a year older than Jerrod and me, but she considered herself much more worldly. I guess she was. She did get around. I don't mean she slept around, or anything like that, but she seemed to pick up and discard boyfriends like old shoes. Personally, if she were to cast her eye on me, I'd run like crazy. That's because I'd been around her enough to look beyond her pretty face to see what she was inside—a pampered, spoiled brat who was always going to expect a heck-of-a-lot more of her dates than they could give.

Luckily, Eileen's bedroom windows had Venetian blinds, which stayed closed tight all day. Once, when we were kicking the soccer ball around like madmen in the hot sun, I thought I saw one of the slats open up a crack, but later, when I ran into Eileen in the kitchen, she didn't say a thing—just gave me one of those nose-in-the-air looks and sniffed. The fact she didn't mind my seeing her in a bathrobe with her hair a mess showed just where I stood in her list of important people—near the bottom.

Jerrod and I had managed, throughout the course of the day, to outfit Pedro with a pretty decent survival kit. He had plenty to eat and drink and things to read. I'd brought him several story books and found a Spanish-language weekly newspaper in the free-literature stacks inside the front door of Kroger's supermarket. We'd pried open a little dirt-encrusted window in the rear of the shed to give him some ventilation, but it was still pretty warm. Pedro seemed to mind less than me or Jerrod, though, so we felt it was going to be all right–until we heard Monday morning's weather report.

"How long is this hot spell supposed to last?" I asked Jerrod.

He leaned back against the end of the lockers and shook his head. "Days. Weeks, maybe. This is normal, you know. Last week wasn't."

"Jeez. Connecticut's starting to look good. I only hope it'll be worth it to have a winter when I don't have to shovel snow."

"Snow? What's that?"

"What passes for brains in your skull, butthead. Anyway, this isn't solving our problem. You're going to have to cut class and do something."

"Me? Why me?"

"Because it's your shed."

"This whole friggin' thing was your idea, not mine. Besides, Einstein, you're the one with the brains. Think of something."

"I just did. You walk out that door, go home, and rescue Pedro."

In the end, we both walked out the door. It was the first time I'd cut classes in my entire history of going to school. Walking to Oakview Terrace and Jerrod's house, I kept looking over my shoulder, expecting to see platoons of soldiers and tanks lined up to prevent my escape. No one noticed us at all.

When we got to the shed, Pedro was gone! Panicked, we raced around the shed and through the garden, heading for the street. As I passed a clump of azalea bushes, I caught a flash of brown that seemed out of place. Turning back, I pushed the bushes apart to find Pedro, lying on his back. His face was dirty and streaked with sweat. It glowed brick red. He didn't respond when I shook him.

"Quick. Let's get 'im into the house."

We half-dragged, half-carried Pedro in through the kitchen and into the bath next to Jerrod's bedroom. I was shaking all over, frightened we hadn't gotten to Pedro in time. He seemed so listless, so lifeless. I ran a tub full of water cool enough to get Pedro's body heat back to normal, but not so cold it would shock him. His jeans and shirt were sticky-wet with sweat, so we dumped him in the tub, clothes and all. He shuddered and screwed up his face, and I realized maybe, just maybe, he was going to be all right.

When we'd stripped off his wet clothes one more time, toweled him off, and dressed him in something dry, we helped him onto Jerrod's bed.

I asked Jerrod, "Would your folks or Eileen come in here?"

"I don't think Eileen would. My mother might, to bring me clean clothes or see if I'd left dirty ones lying around."

"But if you were in your room, would she bust in?"

"Not without knocking. She knows a guy needs a little privacy."

"I wish mine knew that," I said. "The problem is, you can't stay in your room the whole time." I thought a minute. "Your folks always go to work before you leave for school, right?"

"Sure. But don't forget Eileen. We usually go to the bus stop together—unless I'm late and have to walk all the way to school. But hold on. If you're thinking of leaving him here all day, forget it."

Jerrod pulled me out into the hallway, closing the door. "Pedro seems like a nice enough guy, Pete. But we don't know the first thing about him, except we think he's an illegal alien. *Illegal*, get it? What would he have to lose if he decided to grab a few valuables and take off? I'd never be able to explain what happened to my folks."

I had to admit Jerrod had a point. I said, "If we can rest him for just two more days, here in the house where it's cool, maybe that'll be enough so he can leave on his own. We'll have to take turns staying with him."

"What?"

"I'll be sick tomorrow, and you can be sick on Wednesday. Then we'll see. I'll figure out some way to get my mom to let me sleep over here. Then one of us can manage to be in the room all the time. It'll work, Jerrod. It'll work."

Jerrod looked at me for a minute, pursed his lips, and nodded. "Okay, Grayson, okay. You may be a little wimpy in the muscle department, but you do manage to have a useful thought or two, once in a while. That's why I keep you around." He nodded his head a few more times. "It'll work. Yep. You're right, it'll work."

I was glad I'd convinced Jerrod. I wasn't so sure I'd convinced myself. I hate it when I can't convince myself of something.

CHAPTER 8

I spent my day of truancy trying to drag more information out of Pedro. He talked readily enough about his life back in Nicaragua, his village, his parents, his brother and sister. I remembered Managua was the capital of Nicaragua and asked him if he'd been there. He closed his eyes for a second, then shook his head, hard. Clearly, my question about Managua had strayed way too close to whatever he was hiding.

Like almost everyone else in Posoltega, his family had been farmers. Most of what they raised they ate themselves. Some produce, though, mostly sweet potatoes and corn, was sold to provide money for shoes and clothing. There wasn't much money.

Pedro's younger brother Juan had left home once to go to the city and look for work. Within a month he'd come home, near starving. Meager as their life was in the village, at least there was usually food.

"How old is Juan?" I asked.

"He has nineteen years."

"And you?"

"Twenty. Our sister Carlina has seventeen."

"You said Juan and Carlina were with you, gathering wood, when the floods came. Where are they now?"

Pedro's eyes flashed, but he said nothing.

30

"Are they here? In the United States? Are they here with you?" I kept bugging him.

"Yes! Yes, they are here. Now, please, Peter, speak no more of them. Please."

"Sorry, Pedro. I'm just trying to help. I don't understand."

"It is not for you to help. It is I, their brother, who must help them. Not you."

"But . . ."

Pedro rolled over on the bed and turned his face to the wall.

I started to leave, then decided to try again. Maybe if I got him angry, pushed him harder, he'd open up more.

"When we found you in the river, Pedro, you said you couldn't go back."

He shook his head but kept staring at the wall.

"So, tell me, how are you planning to help Juan and—what's her name, Carlotta?—if you don't go back to them?"

"Carlina," Pedro said, in a voice so low I could barely make it out. He turned over and faced me.

"I will go back. I was afraid and I ran away, but I will go back. *Es necesario.* I know it is necessary."

"Tell me about Managua. What happened there? And how'd you get all the way up here?

"*Los Coyotes.*"

"*Los* what?"

"*Coyotes.* That is what they call those men who take much money to bring people to the United States. People from *Mejico* or Central America, like me."

"Where'd you get the money? It must have cost a bundle."

"It cost us nothing."

"I don't understand."

"Juan and Carlina and I—we went to Managua after our parents were gone. We had nowhere else to go."

"What did you do there?"

"We begged. We stole—just a little—to eat, you understand. We were starving."

Pedro put his chin on his chest and said nothing for a long time. I kept quiet, too.

"Many were starving. People were . . . doing terrible things for food. Women, young girls, were offering their bodies . . . men and boys were fighting, even worse."

"I'm sorry, Pedro, I didn't mean to . . ."

"The three of us, at least we had each other. Carlina . . . had two brothers to *protect* her." Pedro laughed, a cold, dry sound.

"And then?"

Pedro sniffed. "And then—the *coyotes* came. There were two of them. They asked us where our family was. We told them we were alone. There were just us three. They looked at each other and smiled."

"So they brought you here for free? They didn't want any money?"

"Oh, no. Someone was paying them. The man we were coming to work for paid them well. A good man, they said. He will give you a bed and food and money for your work."

Pedro snorted another harsh laugh.

I asked, "So who are you working for? Why'd you run away?"

"*No más.* No more. I have said too much. Please ask no more."

"What are you going to do now?"

"I will go back to help my brother and my sister when I can. I was wrong to run away. I am ashamed."

Tuesday night at the Wilsons' was a challenge. Jerrod and I couldn't very well take turns staying in the room during dinner. The Wilsons ate together at the dining room table, and naturally, I was expected to join them.

Normally, the experience of sitting down to a meal as a family would have been a treat for me. Mom and I ate dinner together about half the time; other times our schedules just didn't seem to mesh. Even when we ate together, she'd spend the time ragging on me about something or grilling me about whether I was getting enough sleep, eating nutritious meals, stuff like that. I know mothers are supposed to worry about their kids, but her concern for me was like this heavy woolen blanket, suffocating me.

Dinner at the Wilsons' was a new experience for me. They talked about movies, politics, neighborhood gossip. They joked. Except for Eileen, who kept her nose in the air and acted like she was too refined for all of that foolishness, the Wilsons seemed to enjoy each other. They went out of their way to bring me into the conversation, and it felt so good, until I thought about going home to my normal meals, where the best I could hope for was silence.

I watched Eileen wolfing down her food. Amazing. She's this anorexic-looking thing, but she eats as much as her chubby brother. Go figure. Metabolically speaking, I guess I'm a lot less like my friend Jerrod than his insufferable sis.

Midway through dinner, while I was trying to piss off Eileen by bad-mouthing her latest boyfriend, we heard a loud thump from Jerrod's bedroom. Jerrod gave me a wide-eyed look, but I refused to look back at him. That would've tipped off his parents immediately we were hiding something. Instead, I jumped up before anyone else could and said, "I'll check it out. I left a pile of books on the edge of the desk. Probably fell off."

Pleased with my quick thinking, my mind was still whirling as I went into Jerrod's room. *Is Pedro all right?* I didn't see him at first and closed the door behind me, my heart jumping. Then I spotted a brown elbow on the floor against the wall on the opposite side of the bed. I charged around the end of the bed, expecting to find Pedro unconscious. Instead, he had one arm clasped across his chest to keep it from shaking and his lips were clamped tight so no sound could escape. He was struggling to keep from bursting out laughing!

"*¿Qué pasó?*" I asked. "What's going on?"

"I was trying to look out of the window from the bed and I fell, like a rolling weed."

"A tumbleweed?"

"Yes. A tumbleweed. Giddyup, cowboy."

I didn't have time to explain to Pedro it was the horse, not the cowboy, who needed to giddyup. I helped him back up onto the bed, slowly because his ribs obviously still hurt. I asked him how he felt, and he gave me a palms-in-the-air *What can you do?* gesture.

Starting to leave, I turned back and said, in English, "You know, Pedro? You're one tough hombre." I almost opened the door into the hallway before I realized I'd been gone an awful long time just to pick up a fallen stack of books. I rushed into the bathroom next to Jerrod's bedroom and flushed the toilet. Back at the table, I said, "Sorry. It was the books all right."

Mr. and Mrs. Wilson just nodded and went on with their dinner. Eileen showed she couldn't care less about what I'd said with an extra sniff of her upraised nose. Jerrod smiled at me, and I gave him the briefest wink before applying myself again to my meat and potatoes.

Jerrod and I spent the rest of Tuesday night closed off in his bedroom, after explaining we had "a monumental amount of homework."

"That much?" Mr. Wilson laughed.

Oh, yes," I said. "Prodigious." Looking at Eileen, I said, "That means *a lot*."

"Asshole," said Eileen.

"Eileen!" said Mr. Wilson.

"Good night, y'all," I said, tipping an imaginary hat.

I'd slept for two nights on the floor on a makeshift bed consisting of Jerrod's bedspread and two blankets. When I was younger, I'd been able to sleep soundly on a slab of concrete, but now, every time I turned over I seemed to be all angles, elbows, and hip bones.

Jerrod had two twin beds but it felt wrong to displace their owner, and Pedro needed all the comfort he could get.

As I lay in the dark, thinking over the evening's events, I decided that, all-in-all, it had gone well. I decided that, all-in-all, I'd *done* well. I'd reacted quickly to the emergency of Pedro's falling out of bed. I'd said the right things. Made all the right moves. I'd even gotten in a dig or two at Eileen, in front of and, apparently, with the approval of her parents.

I fell asleep confident all would work out well. Tomorrow I'd go to school, maybe fake a little cough to show how dedicated I was to return so soon after my horrible illness. Jerrod would stay home with Pedro, and tomorrow evening we'd decide if he was well enough to leave.

Things didn't quite work out that way. The school acted quicker than I'd have thought possible, tracking down my mother at work to find out why I hadn't reported for class the previous day. I'd assumed they would let it go, since I was back in school, fake hacky cough and all. I was wrong.

I was called to the office and had to explain to Mom on the phone, in front of God and the principal, that I hadn't called her from the Wilsons' because I didn't want to worry her. That, of course, *really* got her worried and she started grilling me about my symptoms—headache? Sore throat? Tight chest? Coughing? How was my nose? Had I taken any antihistamines? I found myself sweating, like a criminal being interrogated under a klieg light. I needed to admit to symptoms bad enough to have caused a day off, but not so bad I *still* needed to be home. *Here comes this lying stuff again.*

I kept looking at the principal, Mr. Hyatt, who had screwed down one eye and was staring at me like a pugnacious bulldog. No way was he believing this baloney, though I seemed to be winning over my mother. She was always prepared to believe in any calamity, real or imagined, which might befall her only child.

In the cafeteria at lunch time, I sat by myself. With my one close friend not there, I just didn't feel like making the effort to break into one of the groups that seemed to congregate at the same tables every day. I could have easily held my own with the brainy types who had science and engineering careers on their minds. So far, though, I'd avoided them. I had no interest in being labeled. I worked on the school paper, the *Bennington Blade*, and there were one or two fellow journalists I had a decent relationship with. None of them ate lunch the same period, though.

Looking at the tables where the jocks were horsing around and shouting obscenities at each other, I realized I *had* been labeled, though. What's worse, I had been *nicknamed*. "Airball." I heard it in the hallways a dozen times a day. It stemmed from my very first day in gym class when I was handed a basketball by Coach Petit and told to take a free-throw. I had missed the net, the hoop, even the backboard.

Petit looked at me, shaking his head. He said, "Jesus," and then gave the ball to someone else. When the other guys started calling me "Airball," they looked to the coach for his reaction. When they didn't get any, the name stuck. A week later, Petit was calling me "Airball" like all of his disciples. No, there was no way I was going to eat lunch with the testosterone crowd.

I bolted down my food and was bringing my tray to the dirty-dish window when I spotted Jerrod coming in the door. Slamming my tray down, to the annoyance of the kitchen-ladies, I dragged Jerrod off, demanding an explanation.

"What the heck are you doing here? Are you out of your frigging mind, leaving Pedro alone?"

"He's gone."

"He's what?"

"He's gone," Jerrod said, pushing me away. "I think he said he was well now and had things to do. What was I supposed to do, huh? We were going to kiss him good-bye tonight or tomorrow morning anyway, weren't we?"

"Yeah, but . . . did he really look okay? Do you think he'll be all right?"

"I dunno. It sounded like he was saying he was okay, but how would I know? I don't understand Spanish."

"Yeah, but did he *look* all right? Jeez, you don't need to speak a foreign language to notice how a guy looks."

"He looked fine. What's your problem? He looked fine."

"Sorry, man. I didn't mean to get all uptight. It's just he didn't look too good last night and . . . I know it sounds funny to say this, but since we rescued him from the river I feel like we're sorta . . . well, responsible for him, somehow."

"Come off it, Pete. We're sixteen years old. We're kids."

"Yeah, right. Is that what you say to your dad when you're talking about getting a car?"

"That's different."

Since Jerrod's dad hadn't come through with a set of wheels just yet, we did what we always did after school—we walked. We went downtown, slurped something sweet from the Dairy Queen, then headed for home.

I was poking along, rehearsing the symptoms of my recent *illness* for what I knew would be endless discussion at dinner, when I saw a guy who looked like Pedro in the alley behind Main Street. I yelled at him, but he didn't seem to hear me. Maybe it was someone else. When I started up the alley to check it out, I realized that, whoever he was, he'd backed into a doorway and was looking right and left like a scared weasel. It looked like he was waiting for someone. I dropped into the shadows myself to watch.

Within a couple of minutes a Ford F250 pickup truck turned into the far end of the alley and came cruising along, slowly. A real beauty. Metallic gray with a flash of red detailing, and the bright silver whirl of custom hubs. When it got to the doorway it stopped, and the person waiting jumped in. With a squeal of tires the pickup roared down the alley, hesitating just long enough before peeling out into the street for me to see the passenger was definitely Pedro. As the truck flashed by, he recognized me and his mouth flew open. I held my hands up, to ask him what was going on. By then, however, he'd regained his composure and was staring straight ahead. It was clear he had no intention of pointing me out to whoever it was driving the truck.

I felt a little hurt by Pedro blowing me off, but after thinking about it, it made sense. He must have known Jerrod and I would get in trouble if anyone learned about our hiding him. He was trying to protect us.

The closer I got to home, the better I felt. Pedro had found someone else, and he was no longer my responsibility. An exciting but stressful chapter of my life was over. If I could make it through dinner, it'd sure feel good to get back to normal. It didn't take long to remember *normal* wasn't all that terrific, and hadn't been for exactly half my life.

CHAPTER 9

Most people tell me they can't remember their eighth birthday party. I remember mine as clear as a bright spring day in New England, because it was the last real birthday party I've ever had. And because it was the day I learned people we love can die.

I'd gone outside three times before noon to insure the weather was warming enough to have the party in the back yard. The trees behind our house were just budding out, but yellow sunlight was slanting through the branches. I heard the garage door close. Dad was home. All excited, I ran in to ask for help setting up the badminton net. My parents' bedroom door was closed, but I could hear voices. I called out, "Dad. Mom. It's really good outside."

They didn't answer. Instead the voices stopped.

"It's beautiful. It's really, really, really beautiful."

There was still no answer, so I knocked and called out, "Hello?"

The door opened a crack and Dad said, "Not now, Pete. Your mom and I are talking."

"What are you . . ."

"I said not now! Just leave us alone." After a beat, he added, "Go fix yourself some lunch."

The door closed with a snap, but not before I heard the sound of crying. Something was wrong with my mother.

When they came out, they didn't say a thing, but got busy setting up for the party. Dad's lips were clamped tight, like he was mad. Mom kept trying to smile, but it looked painful. Her eyes were rimmed with red.

As soon as some of my friends arrived, my dad disappeared into the bedroom again. Mom helped organize games. We played *Oink* and *Tree Tag*, and Mom showed us how to play *Twister*. For a few hours, I strutted around, enjoying being the center of attention, even though every once in a while I caught Mom with a sad expression she tried to hide when she saw me looking.

When all my friends had exchanged presents for cake and jumped into their waiting parents' cars, Dad came out of the bedroom. He called me into the living room and the three of us sat. Mom was clutching her hands together and staring out the window.

Dad said, "Peter, do you know what cancer is?"

CHAPTER 10

Dad,

I guess maybe you know we're now living in this place called Bennington, Texas. I haven't made any close friends here, except for Jerrod. I keep thinking if we'd only moved to a really big city like Houston, or even Austin or San Antonio, I would have had more people to choose from—more chances to make friends. Thinking like that is stupid, of course. Bennington isn't that small a town. Sure, there are social retards and assholes at Bennington High (more profanity, huh?), like everywhere else. But there are a lot of kids whose only fault is they don't go out of their way to befriend the new guy who'd made it clear he doesn't really need friends.

You might wonder about whether or not I have a girlfriend. Let me tell you, the prospect of having one of those seems about as likely as it would be for Mom to hand me the keys to a new car and say, "Have fun, dear."

I think about girls, of course—think about them all the time. Not as friends, though. I think of them as—well, let's be honest about it, what I think about is sex. Does it shock you to know your little Petey's thinking things like that?

I figure romance and all that emotional stuff is for the movies and for characters in books. I suppose it happens to real people, too, but it sure isn't going to happen to me. What do I have to offer a girl? Fact is, Dad, I've turned into a too-tall, too-skinny, nerdy guy whose mother won't trust him and whose father couldn't— couldn't even stand to live on the same planet with him. But you know all about that, don't you, Dad?

    Pete

CHAPTER 11

An eight year-old memory wasn't the only thing to bring me down from the temporary high I felt getting rid of the responsibility of Pedro. When I reported for last-period gym class the following Monday, I was already prepared to hate it. I wasn't disappointed. Petit had us playing volleyball, one of the worst sports ever invented for someone who doesn't fit into the "team mentality."

I avoid team sports like the black death, whenever I can. I'd gone out for track and was doing well in the longer distances. I wasn't world-class, but I'd run the school's fastest time in the mile that year. It should have raised my standing with Petit, but the fact was he coached only football and basketball, and had no regard for sports that didn't involve pushing and shoving. I loved to run. It was something I could do on my own, and I was good at it.

During gym, teams were normally selected by counting off— one, two, one, two. As we lined up, one of the varsity footballers, Travis Masterson, pushed in next to me and said, loud enough to insure an audience, "Hope you don't mind my snuggling up next to you, Grayson. Just don't get the wrong idea. You're not my type, sweetie. I just wanna make sure you and I aren't on the same team."

While everyone was sniggering at this, another walking jock-strap, Don "Bulldog" Brandon, shoved Travis aside and said, in a

43

ridiculous, high falsetto voice, "Oh, no, you don't. I want to be the one to snuggle up to him."

The two of them shoved and wrestled, while everyone laughed. I stood staring into the bleachers, trying to maintain my cool. Finally, Coach Petit came over and forcibly stood Travis and Bull-dog on either side of me, then grabbed two other guys and stuck them in between us, so both of my tormentors would end up on my team.

The game was a nightmare. Travis kept goading me, "One good thing about volleyball, Grayson, is the size of the net. I'll bet even you could hit a volleyball net."

Bulldog added, "Don't tell him that! The turd-brain probably thinks that's what he's supposed to do, hit the net."

"Think so?"

"Sure. Watch this," said Bulldog. He gave the ball a two-handed shove, straight at my head, and I put my hands up to keep from getting hit. Sure enough, the ball caromed away, bouncing off the bottom of the net before it fell to the ground. Some of the other players hooted and cheered.

"I guess we'll have to stop calling him 'Airball' won't we, now?" said Travis, to more laughter.

The next half-hour was pure agony. Not only Brandon and Masterson, but several other would-be comics kept firing the ball directly at me. They wouldn't loop it toward me so I could bat it on, they rifled it at me. Finally, I started just standing still with my hands at my sides, letting the ball hit or miss me.

It was my standing motionless, not the guys causing the prob-lem, that really frosted Coach Petit. But that was par for the course. The only way I could salvage my pride was to stand and take his verbal abuse along with the physical.

Heading to the showers, I heard someone call my name from the bleachers. It was a female voice, and I realized it belonged to Jennifer James, a girl from my Chemistry class. I looked away quickly and started to hurry on. There was no way I was going to put up with more crapola, and this time from a girl.

"Please, Peter. I just want to talk a minute," she said. "Don't run away."

I stopped and looked up at her. She seemed more concerned than malicious, so I decided to take a chance. While climbing the steps to where she was sitting, I threw my shoulders back and walked as tall as I could. I can walk really tall if I put my mind to it.

Sitting beside her, I faced the gym floor, saying nothing. I studied the uniform pattern of seats stretching right and left in front of me, yet I was painfully conscious of the sound of her breath and a faint odor of perfume. For a minute, neither of us spoke.

Finally she said, "I watched what went on down there."

I nodded, continuing my silent inspection of the bleachers and the polished floor beyond.

"They were terrible."

Another nod from me. She didn't say anything, so I sneaked a glance at her and found her staring at me like I was a lab experiment. I hate it when people look at me like I'm a lab experiment. I tried to decide whether jumping up to leave would make me look more or less foolish than I felt.

She touched my knee with a finger and said, "You were awfully brave."

I jerked my head around to face her. "Wha-what?"

"Putting up with all that."

"I just stood there and took it. How is that being brave? Maybe if I'd have laid a few of 'em out on the ground, busted a few noses . . ."

"That would have been stupid, not brave. For sure, you're not stupid."

"Oh, right. You've been keeping tabs on me in Chemistry."

"Maybe I have."

She looked sincere, but what if she was joking with me, looking for something she and the others could laugh about in the girl's restroom. I said, "What's this really about?"

"Why are you being defensive?"

"I just got kicked around . . ."

"I'm trying to help you . . ."

". . . by a bunch of idiots. I don't need help. I don't want help."
I started to get up.

She jumped to her feet, quicker than me. She shouted, "Maybe
you don't deserve help. Just who do you think you are?"

I settled back down and said, quietly, "I'm the guy no one notices
unless they're calling him names. That's who I am."

Sitting beside me, she said, "I noticed."

I shook my head. "It doesn't make sense. Why would a girl like
you . . ."

"What do you mean, a girl like me?"

"I mean you're so cool. And you're so . . . so pretty."

She laughed. "Guys think pretty means empty-headed."

"No. No. You're pretty *and* smart. That's what makes you cool.
Classy. But me, I'm having trouble just talking to you. I can't believe
I am. It's like one of my dreams . . . except, well . . . never mind."

"Never mind what?"

"Just never mind." There was no way I was going *there.*

Walking downtown with Jerrod later, I casually mentioned I had
talked for a long time with Jennifer James. I didn't mention the
humiliation on the volleyball court that had led to our conversation.

"Isn't she the piece that's going with Danny Simms? Short,
brown hair, a real fox?"

I gave him a dirty look. "She's good-looking and has short,
light-brown hair. I don't know about Danny Simms. She's in my
Chemistry class."

"So she came on to you in the bleachers?"

"Jeez!"

"You came on to her?"

"No, I didn't. Not everyone is as horny as you, fuzz-nuts."

"You mean not everyone is as willing to talk about it."

I looked at Jerrod and laughed. "Strange as it may seem, you're right. I guess that's exactly what I mean."

After I got home, I sat in my room and replayed what had happened in the bleachers. Jennifer had seemed, incredibly, to be worried about me. How had I felt about her? She was beautiful, and I'd be lying if I didn't admit she stirred things up in me. But on top of that, her concern seemed to signal she wanted me as a friend.

Who was I kidding? I was in some kind of fantasy land. The trauma of the volleyball-game-from-hell had addled my brain. I tried to apply myself to my homework, but the picture of Jennifer James kept sticking itself in my face. Out of the blue and totally against my will, I felt a red surge of envy for Danny Simms, a guy I'd never even met.

CHAPTER 12

Dad,

Just after I told you about my dismal prospects for romantic involvement, I met this incredible girl. Just like that—out of no-where she pops up, like those kids' birthday cards you open up and the pictures leap out at you. She didn't leap, of course. That would have scared the hell out of me. She just called me over to where she was sitting—in the bleachers, no less—and talked to me. She actually seemed interested in me.

How do I feel about her? I don't know. Jerrod says it's lust, pure and simple, but that's Jerrod. He thinks hormones are what fuels the world and lubricates it, too. Me, I'm more of a romantic. I really think it's possible I could be friends with this Jennifer—that's her name—without envisioning us together in bed. Then I glance at my lap, and I'm not so sure. Maybe I'm not so different, after all, from Jerrod and the rest of the lesser primates.

Wish I had you here to talk about stuff like this. But then, if you were here, maybe we still wouldn't talk. Come to think of it, I'm storing all these letters to you in one file on my computer so I can get rid of them with one mouse click.

Pete

CHAPTER 13

When it comes to relations with the opposite sex, I'm like a blind man in a snowstorm. My dad was gone while I was still young. Talking to Mom about it would be—well, it's out of the question. I hear other guys talking, of course, but to hear them, women are just machines, sex machines.

Once in a while, I try to remember how my parents were when my father was alive. I couldn't remember anything before those last months after he learned about the cancer and before he took matters into his own hands. Even then, I couldn't picture how they treated each other, only how they were with me.

The day after my eighth birthday party, Dad had gone to work as usual. I was in the front yard waiting for him when he came home. I ran to throw my arms around him, and for just a second he held his arms out to me. Then he jerked them back and stood rigid and straight as I hung on to him, crying.

That was the memory I desperately clung to, pushing to the back of my mind an alternate account I feared might be closer to the truth. In this version, I am the one who draws away, repulsed by an image of my father's body being eaten by the worms of his disease. Terrified and suddenly sickened, I checked my headlong rush and ran to my mother instead. It was her arms that held me and tried to comfort my sobbing. As Mom led me into the house,

I risked this furtive glance at Dad and saw him motionless by the car, staring into space.

A wall formed between my dad and me that grew more unscalable as the months went by. I avoided him as much as I could, and he began shouting at me. He scolded me for eating too fast or eating too slow. My hair was never combed right. My room was never clean enough.

I asked Mom, "Why is Daddy so mean?"

"He's just sad. He can't help it."

"He scares me."

"All we can do is help him."

"Why can't he be happy like he used to be?"

"You know why."

I sobbed and buried my face under her arm. "It's me, isn't it."

"Oh, no, it's not . . ."

"I'll try harder. If you want, I'll try to make him happy."

"Oh, Peter, I don't think you can."

"Why can't it be like it was?"

She put her arms around me and hugged me, but it didn't help.

CHAPTER 14

Every other Tuesday afternoon, Cecelia Sanchez comes to clean house. It isn't something we can afford, but for some reason, my mom insists. I tried to argue I wasn't so busy I couldn't manage to work in some vacuuming and tub-scrubbing.

"Mrs. Sanchez needs the money more than we do," said Mom, "and besides, all that dust and chemicals are hard on allergies."

"I don't have any allergies, Mom."

"How do you think you get allergies? Do you think they just show up in the mail?"

There was no arguing with Mom about health matters. Trying to apply logic wasn't worth a flip when it came to things that might affect the well-being of her son. I gave up, happy enough to get out of tub-scrubbing.

I hurried right home after school Tuesday instead of goofing off with Jerrod. Cecelia was still there, cleaning the little bathroom across the hall from my bedroom. Good. It provided a chance to talk to her without arousing my mother's suspicions.

"Cecelia, you came here from El Salvador, right?"

She nodded her head, and I noticed, perhaps for the first time, flecks of gray were sprinkled through her hair, which was drawn back and fastened with a rubber band. Although her smile welcomed a follow-up to my question, I detected a tightening of her face, a slight squinting of her eyes.

51

"Do you still have relatives there?"

"Cousins, yes. And one sister who is not very close with me. That is all."

"Did they have problems with the hurricane?"

"Everyone in El Salvador has suffered from the hurricane, but no, none of my family lost their homes . . . or their lives. They were lucky. Many thousands died."

"I read about relief efforts here. People donating food and clothing and money."

"This is good. It shows people have good hearts. I try to help my sister as much as I can, though we were never friends as children. But she is family. I am afraid what we do is not enough. How can it be enough when millions are without homes or clean water? Many more will die of the sickness."

"How about Nicaragua?"

"The same. In some places, worse. I have some Nicaraguan friends here, and two have family missing. It is terrible."

"Cecilia," I questioned her, "have there been a lot of people from Nicaragua and El Salvador trying to get into the United States? I mean, people who lost their homes or families in the floods?"

Cecilia tensed. She said, cautiously, "I have heard of such people."

"How can they afford to come here, if they're poor and lost everything they had?"

"Those that have relatives already here may get money from them. But I don't know about such things."

"But if they don't have relatives?"

"There are people who would bring them here and give them jobs."

"Why would they do that? There are already people here that need jobs."

"Because they would work for cheap or . . ."

"Or what?"

"Or worse. I have heard some are kept like . . . I have said too much."

"Kept like what? If they don't like it, why don't they leave?"

"Where would they go? They would be arrested by the government. They would be sent back to where they were starving!"

"Are there people like that around here?"

"I know nothing about such things. Nothing. Please, Mr. Peter, I must finish my work now. It is getting late."

I couldn't sleep that night. I tried to separate Pedro's story from Mrs. Sanchez's hints of terrible things, but they kept coming together. Was it possible Pedro, Juan, and Carlina escaped from one hell to end up in another?

Jerrod and I discussed it the next day.

I said, "I can understand people coming here to work for peanuts, considering what they're coming from. Something is better than nothing."

"Why are you still going on about this?" said Jerrod.

"There was something in what Mrs. Sanchez said, or didn't say," I went on, ignoring him. "Something . . . darker, sinister."

"Yeah, right. Spare me."

"No. I mean it. When I asked her if she'd heard about anybody around here keeping people like slaves, she got shifty and uncomfortable and cut things off. The less she wanted to talk, the worse it sounded."

"I can't understand why *you* want to keep talking about it, oh Cosmic Wizard. Pedro's gone. Like you said yourself—he's someone else's problem now. Not ours. Move along, little dogie"

"I can't help it. I'm starting to worry like my mom. Hell, *that's* a scary thought."

"Look. Pedro left on his own, of his own free will. We didn't put a gun to his head and tell him to get out. You were even afraid he left too soon."

"But where'd he go? He wouldn't talk about how he got here or what he'd been doing. Whatever it was, it had him really, really scared."

"So he moved on, like *you* should do."

I said, "But he *didn't* move on. He went back to whatever—or whoever—he'd been running from in the first place. The guy in the gray Ford truck was someone he knew. I know he went back."

"Why, if he was so scared?"

"One reason. No, two really. His brother and his sister."

CHAPTER 15

For nearly a week, I managed not to think about Pedro, Cecelia Sanchez, or her fears about Central American refugees.

My Uncle Tyler came to visit, and he's the kind of person who resists talking about serious subjects at all costs. How he and my mother can have emerged from the same womb is beyond my comprehension. Where she worries about every little thing that comes along, he thinks life's a carnival. While she can't stand the slightest change in routine, he wants to see and taste and touch everything, sample every ride. He's almost ten years younger than her. Maybe that explains it.

While I hate to admit it, I'm probably more like her than him. Sometimes he scares me with his recklessness and who-gives-a-damn attitude. He lives in Tallahassee, Florida, a town that doesn't seem crazy enough to accommodate him. I guess places, like people, aren't always as easy to describe as you think.

The first thing Uncle Tyler said when he walked in the door, even before "Hi, sis" or "Hello, kid," was "Get on some jeans and a fancy shirt. We're going line dancing."

Mom's arms were extended, ready to give him a hug. She pulled them back and tilted her head. "Excuse me?"

"This is Texas. I want to go line dancing."

We did. Uncle Ty made some phone calls and found a place called *The Sidewinder* where I could make the cut age-wise, just barely. It was way out in the country and back off the road behind some trees. It looked like a huge unpainted wooden box with lean-to rooms and extensions tacked on. It also looked like a strong wind off the Gulf would blow it to Oz or, at the very least, to Kansas.

I have no idea how my uncle actually talked his sister into going to *The Sidewinder*. Who says miracles don't happen any more? He is one persuasive dude. But it took all of his powers of persuasion, and mine, to keep her from turning around and walking out the minute we got there. The problem was the smoke. Even though we were early, the place was already blue with smoke. I can see how she thought we might contract emphysema or something, right on the spot.

Thank God we stayed. Probably I haven't had as much all-out fun in my entire life. A whole bunch of people realized right off we were greenhorns and took us in hand, showing us the steps. We practiced dances called the "Boot-shoe-shuffle" and the "Achy-breakie." Of the three of us, my mother turned out to be the best dancer.

"Mom!" I said. "Where'd you learn to dance? I've never seen you do it before."

"I used to be a great dancer. So was your father. We even won contests."

Now, this was a piece of news. You think you know someone. I didn't have much time to think about it though, because a large woman named Bertie or Gertie had me on the floor and was demonstrating something called (I'm not kidding) the "Tush-push." Of course, with my skinny legs and my big feet, I never did get it down smoothly, but it didn't seem to matter to anyone and after a while, it didn't matter to me, either. I couldn't believe it. For the first time in my life, I was enjoying doing something I wasn't good at.

It was a let-down hanging at home the next night. While Mom was in the kitchen fixing dinner, Uncle Ty and I sat and talked.

"So, kiddo, how have you adjusted to life in the Lone Star State? Making friends?"

"I have a pretty good friend, sure."

"*A* friend?"

"Yeah. One. But a good one."

"I take it you're not the big-man-on-campus yet, huh? Taking your time?"

"I guess you could say that." I waited a beat. "But *I* wouldn't."

"Whatcha mean, kid?"

"I mean, I am who I am. Mom doesn't trust me with anything. She thinks I'm a walking disaster about to happen. Every cold is gonna turn into pneumonia. Every time I bring home a B instead of an A, she thinks I'm secretly doing drugs. And Dad . . ."

"What about your dad?"

"All I can remember is him shoving me away before he . . . before he died. He yelled at me all the time and called me names. He said I was worthless, and you know what? He was right. I wanted to help him so bad, wanted to do something to make things easier for him, but I couldn't. I couldn't."

Uncle Tyler shook his head. "Not your fault. He had no right to treat you that way. I can guess why he acted like he did, but he still had no right."

"Why, Uncle Ty? Why'd he do it?"

He stared at me a long time; I knew he understood what I was really asking about.

"He had cancer. You know that. Terminal cancer."

"But he might have lived for a long time. Sometimes people do."

"He was depressed. It's not something I can understand."

"I tried to help him, but I couldn't. Nothing I did helped."

"How could it?"

"I felt like I wasn't good enough. I was . . ."

"Bull ca-ca. You were eight years old. It was the cancer. Not you, not your mom, the cancer. Have you ever considered his pushing you away might have been because he loved you? In some sick, misguided way, he was putting some distance between you, so at the end you wouldn't be filled up with grief for him. Maybe he thought being angry at him would be better for you than mourning him."

My mind whirled. Was it possible? Could he be right? It was an incredible idea, so unbelievable I wanted to toss it in the trash, except coming from Uncle Ty, I had to give it some weight.

Then reality hit me, and I said, so quietly he had to lean forward to hear me, "Yeah, right. I could tell from the blood how much he loved me."

I drifted off in a daylight version of the dream that had haunted my nights for eight years—hearing the gunshot, running down that long hallway, opening the door on . . .

Uncle Tyler had his hand on my shoulder, shaking me. "Hey, Pete. It's all right. It's okay now."

"Sorry."

"You're right, you know. He probably loved you in some crazy, screwed-up way, but in the end, he blew it. I can forgive him almost anything. How he treated you, how he treated your mom. But allowing you to find his body, *that* I will never forgive. Never. Now, where can we find a rodeo?"

"What?"

"Where can we find a rodeo? This is Texas. I want to go to a rodeo."

I started to laugh. At first, Uncle Tyler pretended to be offended, but he was obviously straining to hold it in. Just as I stopped laughing, he snorted and I was off again. This time he couldn't stop himself and before long we were rolling around on the floor, totally out of control.

Through my tears, I caught a glimpse of something blue and realized it was a pair of slacks, worn by a scowling woman standing in the doorway with her hands on her hips.

"What in the world is going on?"

"We're having an in-depth discussion . . . about life," said Uncle Ty. "Come on down and join us."

Mom gave us a dismissive wave of her hand, shook her head, and turned away muttering. "Children. They're all children. Even the big ones."

We didn't make it to any rodeo. I used to think those bumper stickers that read "Shit Happens" was just a clever saying. Now I know it means bad things can really, really happen to you even if you're just minding your own damn business. True enough, I guess, but most of the time we do the things that create our own troubles. And when you wade into it slowly, you don't even realize it until you're waist deep in smelly, brown stuff.

CHAPTER 16

Dad,

Let me tell you about this nightmare I've had, year after year, night after night. I still do, once in a while. In the dream I'm running through a long hallway. At the end is a door, and I know behind it is my father, you. You need me, and I desperately need to get to you, but the door is stuck shut. I pound on it, crying and crying. Then it opens and there you are, lying on the floor. A huge pool of blood is spreading out from your head, which is partly missing. The gun is there. Blood is sprayed all over your desk and on the wall. It's mixed with little specks of something pink. I say, "Please, Daddy . . ." and then I wake up. Even now, I wake up crying.

You hear what I'm saying, Dad? I'm sixteen frigging years old, and I wake up crying. If I hear sirens in the night, like the ones that came to take you away, I wake up sweating.

Uncle Ty was here. He's not the boy you probably remember, though in some ways he probably is. Sometimes I seem older than him, like he's the kid and I'm the grownup. It feels weird.

He has this strange theory, though, about why you kept shoving me away the year before you died—why you kept yelling at me all the time and making me cry. I guess you remember that, right? Ty says you might have figured if I was mad at you, I wouldn't feel so sad. Well, guess what? If that's what you had in mind, it sure-as-hell didn't work.

Have to break off now. I've got to call Jerrod. Things to tell him. I'd tell you, but truth is, I'm not in the mood right now. Maybe some other time.

Pete.

CHAPTER 17

When I saw the metallic gray Ford again, no alarm bells went off—only surprise at seeing it in the school parking lot. It was a pretty flashy machine, and I'd never noticed it before, so I figured it was new. After school I decided to hang around the lot to see who was driving it.

"Whatcha doing, Peter?" a female voice asked.

I turned to see Marlene Briggs, a girl from a couple of my classes. "Nothing," I stammered. "Just waiting for someone."

She giggled and said, "I'll bet I know who."

"What?"

"Like, Jennifer, maybe?"

"Jennifer? Jennifer James?"

"Peter! You're, like, you know . . . blushing. That's so you. That's, like, so sweet." She flashed a huge grin, and swished off to her car, leaving me standing there with my mouth hanging open. Where the hell had that come from? Had Marlene seen Jennifer and me sitting together in the bleachers? I didn't think so. I hadn't noticed anyone around, but I hadn't been in a mood to pay that much attention. Someone might have seen us.

Jeez, I hope she doesn't spread this all over the school. The last thing I need is for Danny Simms to come gunning for me. Then I had an even worse thought. What if Jennifer heard the rumors and

62

thought I was the one spreading them? I could never look her in the face again. Whatever sympathy she had for me from my ordeal on the volleyball court would be gone in a flash.

Worries about Jennifer disappeared when I saw, coming toward me, one of my chief tormentors from that infamous game, Travis Masterson. He had his arm around Heather Barnes, whose breast size almost equaled her reputation as one of Bennington High's easy lays. She was holding onto Travis with both arms as they threaded their way through the parking lot. Travis's younger brother Tony trailed behind. Travis made a point of angling his walk through the parking lot so he would pass through the narrow space where I was standing between two cars. He thrust Heather aside roughly and then elbowed me, shoving my hip against a door handle.

"Sorry, Airball," he said with a smirk. "Didn't see you there. You need to put on some weight."

Travis swaggered away, signaling Heather to follow. She hesitated, looking hurt, but quickly brightened and skipped after him. When they'd reconnected, Travis turned to see me nursing my sore hip. He laughed—a high, harsh, very unfunny laugh. Tony shot me a pleading look and then stared at the ground, clearly embarrassed. *At least assholism doesn't run in the family.*

I watched them work their way through the parking lot for a minute, then turned back toward the school to see who else might be coming. I was a spy, after all, and needed to keep my mind on my mission. When I glanced back at the Masterson brothers, I was surprised to see them stop at the gray pickup. Travis got into the driver's seat and leaned across to unlock the door for Heather and Tony. Tony barely had time to get his door closed before his brother gunned the engine with a roar and took off in a squeal of rubber.

I headed for home to call Jerrod. I'd discovered who drove the truck that picked Pedro up in the alley. I didn't realize the shit had started to happen. Had I been more observant, I might have noticed my shoes were getting a bit sticky and there was a nasty stench in the air.

CHAPTER 18

Jerrod wasn't home when I called. Eileen answered the phone with a bored, "Yeah?"

I should have pretended I was someone important, but I wasn't quick enough.

"Hey, Eileen, put your scuzzy brother on, would you?"

"My scuzzy brother isn't here."

"Tell him I called, will you? Have him call me back."

"Who do you think I am? I'm not your social secretary." She hung up.

"I love you too, Eileen," I said to the buzzing phone. *What a witch.*

I phoned the Wilsons' house again an hour later and was relieved to hear Mrs. Wilson's pleasant voice. She told me Jerrod was still out. He and his father were car shopping.

"For Jerrod or for Mr. Wilson?"

I held my breath and got the answer I was hoping for. "Why, for Jerrod. I assumed he told you."

"I guess he wanted to surprise me."

In fact, it wasn't hard to look surprised when Jerrod came tooling up our driveway later that evening and leaned into the horn. When I went out, he was sitting there beaming through the open window of a brand new Firebird. It was red. Bright red. Fireplug red.

Happy as I was for him, a quick wave of jealousy washed over me. A picture of my beat-up old bicycle came to mind, but I managed to shake it off. I jumped in beside Jerrod, thinking how cool I was going to look, cruising around town in the passenger seat of this awesome set of wheels.

He backed out of the driveway and revved the engine. "Two hundred horses in this baby. What do you think?"

"I think I have to ask you a favor. Please drive slow when you're anywhere, *anywhere* near my house. My mom's gonna go apeshit at the thought of me even getting into this machine."

"Done, my man." Jerrod crept to the corner until he was out of sight of my house, then floored it.

After I'd caught my breath, I managed to croak something about not wanting to decorate a telephone pole this early in the evening. Jerrod slowed down as we hit downtown.

"Besides, in case you hadn't noticed, this is a red car," I said. "Cops always pay special attention to red cars. Now I know why."

We pulled into the new Sonic and ordered milkshakes through the speaker. When the attendant brought our order, Jerrod was disappointed she wasn't anyone we knew. He kept looking around, hoping for some recognition, but the place was filled with strangers.

"Guess we'll have to cruise Main Street," he said. "Nothing beats driving in circles, looking at girls."

"Don't give me that line of bull. What you want is for girls to be looking at you."

Jerrod flashed me an impish grin. "Maybe that, too."

We drove the strip twice each way and did get a few waves and a lot more stares from the Bennington High kids who were doing the same thing. As we were making another turn, using Kroger's parking lot, I saw Travis Masterson's Ford pickup turning onto Main.

"There he is," I shouted. "I called you earlier. I found out who drives the truck that picked up Pedro. It was Travis Masterson. See it over there, the gray and red one?"

"He's heading out of town," said Jerrod. "What say we follow him?"

"Out of town? He'd see us."

"I'll hang way back. Like they do in the movies."

"Undercover cops don't drive red cars, even in the movies."

"Sure they do. In Miami and Hawaii."

I didn't even try to point out the obvious idiocy of that statement. Instead, I settled back in my burgundy leather bucket seat. We followed Travis, staying as far back as possible while keeping his taillights in view. He made a right then a left on an even narrower country road, pulling into the driveway of a farmhouse.

"Drive on by," I said. "If we stop, he'll know we were following him."

As we passed the driveway, we could see Travis bounding up the front porch.

"Did you see the name on the mailbox?" asked Jerrod.

"Nope. It's getting kinda dark. Besides, I was watching Travis."

"It was Brandon."

We looked at each other and then said, simultaneously, "Bulldog."

"Makes sense," said Jerrod. "He and Travis are best buds."

"Pull off over there," I commanded.

"What for?" Jerrod slammed on the brakes and spun into a little side road.

"Travis left the lights on in his car. That means he's leaving again right away. Either he's dropping something off or he's picking Bulldog up."

"You think?"

"Guar-an-teed."

We pulled in behind a row of trees, shut off the lights and waited. From our vantage point, we could just make out several dull yellow rectangles where light from the Brandon house filtered through curtained windows. We could also see the red pin-prick glow from the gray pickup's taillights. Soon, the taillights were joined by a white reversing light, and the pickup backed down the driveway.

"He's on his way," I said. "Get ready to haul ass."

"Not to worry, ol' buddy. It's under control." Jerrod gunned the engine briefly then let it settle back into a quiet idle.

Instead of heading back into town as we expected, Travis started up the road, passing directly in front of our hiding place. As he turned, his headlights swept across the grove of trees where we waited. We instinctively ducked our heads and stayed scrunched down until the pickup had passed.

"Do you think he spotted us?" I asked nervously, as we pulled out onto the roadway.

"Nah. Besides, even if he did, he'd have probably thought we were some couple making out."

"Sorry to disappoint you, big boy, but you're not my type."

"Shucks. I guess we'll just have to go back to sleuthing."

It was getting late. Lights from occasional farmhouses glimmered in the distance. They grew further and further apart until the only break in the blackness was a pale half-moon, the glow of our headlights reflecting off cracked pavement, and two tiny red lights far ahead. The truck's taillights moved to the left and disappeared. When we reached the same spot, the road turned, running parallel to a narrow arroyo where moonlight glimmered off the rippled surface of water.

"I think that's Diablo Creek," I said. "Last time we saw it was down by the Brazos under the flood. We couldn't even tell where it came in."

"Still running kinda high."

"Seems like."

Travis's taillights disappeared again. It was pitch dark now. A chill went through me. Our quarry's taillights had made me feel more comfortable—a small sign of human contact in this black emptiness.

A barricade with reflector arrows showed a sharp right turn in the road, toward the river. Afraid we would lose Travis, Jerrod accelerated around the turn and up the ramp of a hump-backed bridge spanning the creek. There was a queasy sensation in my gut—the same feeling you get when you're on a roller-coaster heading up that first incline and you know once you get to the top, your quiet world is about to get swept away.

As we came over the top, Jerrod slammed on the brakes, fishtailing to a stop. On the down-slope beyond the bridge, a metallic gray Ford F250 blocked the center of the road. Travis Masterson and Bulldog Brandon stood in front with their arms folded across their chests. If they were concerned about who was following them, they didn't show it. They stood with their feet spread apart like gunfighters poised for a showdown.

I expected Jerrod to throw it in reverse and get the hell out of there. Instead he sat with his chin down and his hand shading his eyes. After a minute, he said, "We've gotta face them."

"Why?"

"They know this is my car, or they will. I don't want to live with this hanging over my head. Let's go."

"Jeez, Jerrod. Out here in the dark in the middle of nowhere? It's nuts and . . . they'll kick our butts from here to . . ."

Jerrod opened his door and got out of the car. I sighed and followed him. There wasn't much else I could do. We walked toward Travis and Bulldog, or rather Jerrod walked and I trailed behind. Bulldog was squinting and Travis was peering through shaded eyes to see who was approaching. I realized we had the glare of Jerrod's headlights directly behind us.

Travis growled, "You've got some explaining to do." He stepped forward and grabbed Jerrod by the shoulders and spun him around so his face was in the light.

"Wilson!" said Travis. "I should've known it would be some idiot like you." He turned and grinned at me wickedly. "And if this is Wilson, that little pussy over there has got to be Airball."

I stepped forward. "Hey, Travis. How's it going?"

"I can't believe this." Travis snorted. "Bulldog, can you frigging believe this? These little creeps tail us halfway across Texas to ask us 'How's it going?' like we're at some hinky Junior-Senior prom. How's it going!"

Bulldog grabbed the front of my shirt with both hands, lifting me up. He probably carries two-hundred pounds to my one-forty. I flailed my arms, struggling, but without being able to plant my feet firmly, it didn't do much good.

"You wanna fly, Airball? You're gonna have to flap your little wings better than that."

Travis was talking to Jerrod. "Give me some kind of clue, turd burger. Why are you following us? What are you up to? The curiosity's killing me."

Jerrod turned to look at me. I shrugged. My mind was working like crazy, but I hadn't come up with anything that made sense. I stammered, "We were out for a ride in the country. Any law against that?"

"Bull. You followed me from town and hid behind the trees till we left Bulldog's. I wanna know why you're following us. Right now, if you value those pretty teeth."

"Okay. Okay," Jerrod confessed. "You're right. We were following you, but we didn't know it was you. I mean we didn't know who was in the truck. It's just that Pete saw you in the alley picking up . . ."

Travis spun toward me. Panicked, I interrupted with, "We were looking to follow someone, anyone. Just for kicks—trying out Jerrod's new car. You know when you get something new? Anyway,

I saw this good-looking truck, and I thought it would be good to follow, being as it was so cherry and all."

"Yeah, right. What about hiding in the damn bushes? Huh?"

"We saw you'd left your lights on so we knew you—I mean who-ever was driving—would be taking off again. Waiting just made it all the more exciting."

Travis stood there, gears turning in his brain. It looked like he was just about to shrug us off and back down when something changed his mind. He picked up a rock and started for Jerrod's car.

"You want exciting? I'll show you exciting."

Jerrod shouted, "No." He ran after Travis but Bulldog tackled him from behind. I stood paralyzed with uncertainty.

Travis walked once around the car, swinging his arm like he was trying to find a good spot to bash the rock. He stepped back and aimed a sidearm fast ball at the windshield.

Jerrod moaned, "Noooo . . ."

The rock whistled harmlessly over the Firebird's roof and splashed into Diablo Creek. Travis shrieked with laughter. He swaggered back to his truck, and he and Bulldog jumped in. Travis executed a three-point turn, then stuck his head out the window and shouted back at us. "So long, pussies. Have a nice night."

Jerrod and I stood in the roadway, listening to the retreating sounds of maniacal laughter. I was thinking what a wuss I'd been, standing there frozen in fear. I hate it when I'm frozen in fear.

CHAPTER 19

We started back to town. For once, Jerrod was driving slowly and carefully. I think he'd realized, as Travis held the rock over the windshield, the Firebird was made of metal, paint, and glass, capable of being damaged or destroyed.

I said, "I tried to stop you telling them about Pedro."

"Why?"

"I don't know. A bad feeling. Why would Pedro have left with someone like Travis Masterson?"

Jerrod shrugged. "How would I know? You're the one with all the bright ideas."

"Notice the operative word is 'bright,' unlike your dumb-ass ideas. 'Oh, let's follow that truck'. Come to think, it was you who said, 'Oh, let's go down to the river and watch the flood.' That's how this whole thing got started, remember?"

"Get out, Grayson."

"What?"

"Get out. That's your house, isn't it?"

"Uh. Yeah. We're here already?"

"Time flies when you're messing your britches. Sweet dreams, pussycat."

"You sound like Travis."

"Nah. *He* was just kidding." Jerrod laid rubber as he drove off. I ran around and sat on the back steps to delay going into the house for a few minutes. There was no way I was going to have Mom connect my arrival home with the squealing of hot tires. *There I go again. My bravery is really overwhelming.*

The next morning, as I ate my Frosted Mini-Wheats, I wondered whether I would be taking the bus to school or riding with Jerrod. In all the excitement of last night, we'd forgotten to discuss that most important little item. The phone rang, and I ran to pick it up, sure it was Jerrod. It was, but I barely recognized the voice behind the shouting.

"They did it. The creeps were too chicken to do it with us there so they come sneaking around in the middle of the night . . . . Oh, man . . . I can't believe it. Even cretins like that, how could they?"

"Hold on. Hold on. How could they what? What happened?"

"My tires! The assholes slashed my tires."

"How do you know it isn't just a flat?"

"All four of them? Let me tell you this, man, there's one gray Ford pickup that's in a heap of trouble."

"No, Jerrod! Don't start a feud. You can't win."

"*Who's* starting it?" Jerrod's voice rose again. "Who's starting it? I didn't slash my own frigging tires."

"I know, I know. But you don't know for absolute sure who did."

"What? Do you have any doubt?"

"No," I had to admit, "but there's such a thing as proof. We don't have any. And that's not the point. Listen to me. You try to get back at them, then they get back at you. And no offense, Jerrod, but you'd lose. These are tough *hombres*. I wouldn't put it past them to go from slashing tires to bashing skulls."

"But I can't just do *nothing*."

"You can go to school and act like it never happened. If you see them, look cheerful. That'll frost their buns more than anything."

Jerrod was silent for a long time, so I added, "Look, you're always talking about my being Einstein and all that. Well, trust me on this one. Please."

I hung up the kitchen phone. Uncle Tyler came staggering out of the living room, rubbing his eyes. "Hey, man, whazzup?"

During his visit he'd been sleeping on the convertible couch, except for the nights I stayed at Jerrod's. While he made himself a cup of instant coffee, I filled him in on Jerrod's call. Of course, I didn't mention the events of the previous night. I just said Jerrod had very good reason to suspect Brandon and Masterson.

Uncle Tyler said if he'd been my age, he'd have gotten back at the nasties for sure, but now that he'd reached the ripe old age of twenty-six, wisdom had set in, and he had to agree with my advice to Jerrod.

"How'd you get to be so wise so young?" he asked.

"I guess I learned what not to do by watching you."

"Smart. Very, very smart."

"Uncle Ty?"

"Uh, huh?" he murmured, between caffeine slurps. "And by the way, since you're so wise for your years, why don't you dispense with the 'Uncle' bit. I used to get a kick out of being an uncle when I was ten. The novelty's worn off."

"Okay, Auntie Tyler, here's my question."

"Smartass."

"What I want to know is, am I really being smart, or am I being a wuss? You know me. I've always backed away from anything unpleasant. When I was a kid, I'd walk an extra three blocks to avoid a barking dog, even one behind a fence. And now, I hardly have friends 'cause, I dunno, I figure if I try to make friends, people'll turn me down. I can't stand the thought of that."

"What about your bud, Jerrod? You got him."

"I know. It's strange. I can't figure that one."

"How many close friends does Jerrod have, besides you?"

"None, I guess."

"Do you see an answer to your question in there, some-where?"

I thought for a minute. I could see what Ty was suggesting.

"One more question. If Jerrod doesn't do anything, do you think Travis and Bulldog will let it drop? Or will they, you know, up the ante?"

"I'm not sure, kid, but my guess is it's the only chance your friend's got. If it's all-out war, my gut tells me a guy named Bulldog is going to play to win."

By this time I was definitely late for school. Ty called after me as I was dashing out the front door, telling me he wouldn't be home that night. He was heading over to San Antonio for a couple of days.

"This is Texas," he explained. "I need to meet me some *señoritas* along the River Walk. Place is thick with them, or so I'm told."

"The only *señoritas* you're likely to meet are tourists from New Jersey, walking with their parents and their little brothers."

"Hey, I'm not particular."

"Yeah, but *they* might be, in which case . . ." By this time I was in full gallop. I'd already tarnished my spotless record by cut-ting classes for a full day. I didn't want to add "tardiness" to my résumé.

I spent the day avoiding what seemed like half the people in the school. I wasn't eager to run into Travis, Bulldog, or any of their jock-strap buddies. Last-period Phys Ed was going to be a problem; I'd face that when the time came.

Jennifer James and her friends also had to be avoided, though for an entirely different reason. If, as a result of our talk in the bleachers, there were rumors about Jennifer and me floating around, well, I just couldn't handle it. It was way too embarrassing. Worst of all was how guilty I'd look. I felt guilty, not for anything I'd done, but for what I was feeling. Since we'd talked, I thought about Jennifer all the time—before school, during boring lectures, even at night. *Especially* at night. There was no way I could face Jennifer. One look at me, and she'd know, guar-an-teed.

The first test came when I passed Marlene Briggs walking with Danny Simms in the hallway. Talk about irony. The rumor-monger and the injured boyfriend together. I tried to pretend I didn't see them, but Marlene speared me with her high-pitched squeal. "Peter! You're so in a hurry. You're, like, always so in a hurry."

I wanted to sink into the floor.

Marlene chattered non-stop. "I guess you know Danny, don't you? Of course you do. I mean, like, this isn't that big of a school, and . . . why, Peter, you're, like, blushing again. Do you always go around blushing?"

"Overheated," I stammered. "You're right, I get to rushing around and I get . . . well, overheated."

"That's, like, so *you.*"

"That's me all right, I guess." I looked over at Danny Simms, preppy in a button-down collar and a jacket with maroon and white school colors. He was shuffling his feet and staring at the ceiling, looking bored. At least he didn't seem angry. *He hasn't heard the rumors yet. Give it time. He will.* Like Marlene said, Bennington wasn't *that* big a school.

I survived gym by not going. Reaching into my bag of clever tricks, I took advantage of my third period English teacher, Mrs. Larson, who also was faculty adviser for the school newspaper.

"I've got a deadline problem," I told her. "I have to finish two articles for this week's *Blade* before I go home. But my mom is working late tonight, and I'm going to have to head home right after school. I've got to cook dinner and do a bunch of other work." I figured, correctly, Mrs. Larson would be a sucker for that line— working single mom and all that.

"Would you be able to write me a pass from Phys Ed, last period? We're not doing anything special today, track I think, and since I run track all the time . . ." I trailed off, hopefully.

It worked. I got my pass and a load of guilt to go with it. Man, was I becoming an accomplished liar. I was going to have to reform, or I'd end up getting myself into something I couldn't talk my way out of.

Back home, I scooped up the *Bennington Times-Sentinel* from the front walkway. Its plastic wrapper was tamale-hot and sticky from a day in the sun. *Better work on my articles for the* Blade. *Not before a snack, though.*

At the kitchen table with a peanut butter and mayonnaise sandwich, a specialty of mine, and a can of orange soda, I leafed through the *Sentinel*. People killing each other in Afghanistan, stupid stuff out of Washington, politicians in Austin shaking hands and beaming for the camera. Every day was the same boring stuff.

On the third page of the local news section, a short article caught my eye. I read it twice, in disbelief.

Body Found in Diablo Creek.

The body of an unidentified, young Hispanic male was discovered in Diablo Creek yesterday afternoon. It was first spotted by Jacob Scolaris of Bennington, while he was fishing from the Highway 497 bridge.

The article went on to describe the dead man as 5' 6" tall, weighing a scant one-hundred pounds, with long, dark brown hair. He was shirtless and shoeless, wearing only tattered jeans. No identification was found on the body, and the sole distinguishing feature was a thin, three-inch long scar on his forehead. An autopsy was planned.

My hands were trembling as I set the paper aside. Pedro. The body in the creek was Pedro. Or maybe not. I tried to convince myself it could be anybody. Probably lots of Hispanics have long, thin scars on their foreheads. The fact I had never met one didn't mean there weren't any. *Who am I kidding?* The dead man had to be Pedro.

"Do you think we ought to tell the police what we know?" I asked Jerrod, showing him the paper.

"What point would it serve? There's nothing we can do for Pedro now. What's the use of getting involved?"

"I was just asking," I said. "You're probably right. We don't know anything about where he's been. Not for sure anyway." I added, "Or why he had a habit of swimming in dangerous waters."

Jerrod shook his head.

"Jerrod?"

"Yeah?"

"I'm pretty broken up about this."

"Me, too."

"Pedro was older than us, but he'd needed our help, and when we were helping him, it seemed like he was younger, just a kid. He'd been through so much, you know? The hurricane, his parents. Jeez, I feel bad, like we failed him, somehow."

"Yeah, but we didn't, Pete. We helped him, gave him food and a bed. And friendship. Don't forget that, we gave him our friend-ship."

"I know, I know. But, Jerrod?"

"Yeah?"

"It wasn't enough. Whatever Pedro was running from, in the end it got him. Bottom line, Jerrod: We failed him, it got him."

CHAPTER 20

The next day, Jerrod and I were leaving the cafeteria when Jennifer caught my sleeve and spun me around.

"Peter, can we talk?"

"I . . . I'm late for class." *Here it comes.*

"Not now. After school. I know you stop off at Dairy Queen. Let's talk there."

This was exciting, but embarrassing, too. Am image floated into my mind of her bawling me out for bragging about us around school. I could picture people in the booths on either side, stopping their talk, tilting their heads, straining to hear what she was saying. I could feel myself pressed into the seat as she ground her heel into my soul, and wishing she wasn't so beautiful.

I almost broke into a run. "Sorry. Busy," I shouted over my shoulder as I hurried off, Jerrod puffing to keep up.

"What was that about? Why'd you blow her off?"

"I'm busy."

"You hurt her feelings."

"Nope."

"You did. I could tell. You hurt her feelings."

Jerrod didn't understand. How could he? He had no way of knowing how Marlene and her stupid rumors had exposed me to Jennifer's anger. I tried to argue more about it as I bounded down the steps leading to the athletic fields. My explanations were cut off by the crash of a shoulder that sent me reeling into the handrail.

It was Travis Masterson. He stood rubbing his elbow and working himself up to act mad.

"Watch where the hell you're going, Airball."

"You did that on purpose," I said, massaging my shoulder, realizing as I said it I sounded like a four-year old. I wasn't even sure it was true.

True or not, Masterson was intent on showing his toughness to me and to everyone around us. "I'll show you on-purpose, you little pea-brain," he said, grabbing me by the shirt-front and shoving me backwards across the rail. I thought my back was going to snap. I broke loose and rolled face down; shoving the guardrail with both hands, I slammed my body back into Travis. He slipped on a step and went down, grabbing my leg as he fell. The two of us rolled together down the last three steps, arms and legs flailing in every direction.

"Fight," someone yelled. The refrain was picked up by an excited chorus of voices. Travis was beating at me with both fists, and I was thrashing back. It was a free-for-all, like two cats in a barrel, scratching and biting. We rolled across the walkway. We flattened a boxwood hedge and landed on the lawn. For a minute, I felt sun-dried grass pressing into my cheek and eyeball, and then I was on top, arms pumping, completely out of control.

I felt myself being lifted up bodily, gripped tightly from behind. I continued to punch and kick wildly until I realized I was slicing thin air. I was turning my head to see who held me when Travis, taking advantage of the situation, came off the ground in a single motion like some kinda madman and plowed his fist deep into my stomach. The pain was worse than awful and so sudden I couldn't breathe. I doubled over in agony. Still being held from behind, I raised my legs up, throwing whoever held me off balance. He dropped me, and I curled up on the ground, barely conscious someone was speaking.

"What's going on?" Through the haze of pain, I recognized Coach Petit's voice.

"He started it!" Travis said, sounding as childish as I had a few minutes earlier.

Jerrod spoke up. "No, he didn't. Masterson started it. Bumped into Pete and tried to throw him off the stairs."

"You're Wilson, aren't you?" said Coach Petit. "Grayson's buddy."

"That's right."

"So, we have only your word against Masterson's. And you're Grayson's good buddy. Anyone else see what happened?" he asked the onlookers crowding around. No one answered. Petit nudged me with his toe and said, "That your story, too, Airball. What do you have to say?"

I couldn't say anything. I croaked something unintelligible.

"Gawdalmighty," said the coach. He half helped, half dragged me to my feet, where I stood, wobbly and still bent over in pain.

"C'mon, Masterson. You and the little pussy and I are going to Principal Hyatt's office. Let him get to the bottom of it."

We walked, actually they walked and I limped, to the principal's office. I could feel the curious stares of the crowds that parted and regrouped as we passed. The offices were at the far end of the school, and the journey seemed to go on for miles. I collapsed into a chair in the secretary's area and Travis stood by the window, while the coach went into the inner sanctum. When he came out, he jerked his head backwards and said, "Okay, boys, you're on. Have fun." He grinned at me as I stumbled into the principal's office.

Principal Hyatt was seated at his desk, watching the door as we entered. He leaned forward with his elbows pressed into the desktop and his index fingers pressed into his chin. With his round face and steady gaze, he looked like an owl preparing to surprise a field mouse with a swift deployment of slashing talons.

A sitting area was at the other end of the room. It held a small couch, a wing-back chair, and a wooden coffee table perched on an oriental rug. It was supposed to look homey and comfortable and all that. Now, though, all the oriental rugs in the world couldn't make up for the double dose of anger and humiliation I felt. Hyatt told Travis and me to sit on the couch. I scrunched over into the corner farthest from Travis. The principal pulled a hard-backed visitor's chair over from his desk and sat squarely across the coffee table from us. His short, stout body filled the chair completely. His face was flushed, giving the impression he'd just completed a ten-mile jog instead of a walk across the room.

His first words were hardly reassuring. "Well, Travis," he said. "How's your father doing? I haven't seen him in weeks."

I groaned inwardly.

"He's just fine, sir. Busy, as usual."

The principal laughed. "I doubt if I'll ever see the day when Oliver Masterson isn't busy. How he finds the time for all he does . . . well, we're getting off the subject." He turned to me. "So, Grayson."

"Yes, sir?"

"Coach Petit says you started a fight with Masterson here. Considering the fact he's so much bigger than you, that strikes me as rather ill-advised."

"But I didn't. It was him. He tried to throw me off of the steps."

"Don't try to weasel out of this, Grayson. You'll just make it worse. The coach was an eyewitness, remember."

"The coach wasn't even there! He didn't come until later. All he knows is what Travis told him—and me, and he'd never believe me."

Principal Hyatt took off his glasses and rubbed his eyes with fleshy, stubby fingers. Without his glasses, dark circles seemed to frame eyes that were tired and cold. I was relieved when he put the glasses back on.

He sighed. "I'd just like to know why," he said, continuing to look at me.

"I told you, I didn't start it. I had no reason to start it and I didn't."

"Perhaps I'm asking the wrong person. Masterson? Why do you think Grayson did this?"

"Beats hell out of . . . it beats me, sir. I have no idea. I was just heading up the stairs and, pow!"

"Well, it's obvious I'll get no further with this inquiry." He stood abruptly and moved to the door. Opening it, he motioned us through. "Grayson, I'm going to let you off lightly this time. Consider yourself on probation. But one more incident, and you'll be suspended. Understood?"

I refused to look at him or to answer. I nodded my head slightly. When I did look up it was to see Jerrod, jumping out of a visitor's chair and advancing toward us.

"Mr. Hyatt," he was saying. "I don't know what's happening here, but Pete didn't do anything wrong. It was Travis."

"Nice try, but I've had the story from Coach Petit." He turned away, and Jerrod caught his sleeve.

"Mr. Hyatt . . ."

The principal jerked his arm away and turned on Jerrod, menacingly. "What's behind this? What's going on? I demand to know why you persist in . . ."

Jerrod flung his hand toward Travis. "He . . . he's been threatening us. He slashed the tires on my car. He . . ."

"He what?"

"I did not. What the hell is he talking . . ."

"He slashed the tires on my car. My brand new car."

"Just when did this happen?" asked the principal.

"Night before last, in the middle of the night. He came sneaking around, him and his buddy Brandon." He shot Travis a look that would turn plums into prunes.

"Back in here," said Principal Hyatt, "all three of you. Now!"

As we stood around the edges of the oriental carpet, shuffling our feet, Hyatt marched to his desk, consulted his rolodex, and dialed the phone.

"Oliver. Bill Hyatt here. How are things? . . . Oh, fine. Tony? No, not Tony. It's about Travis. He got into a bit of a scuffle, but he's fine, not to worry . . . no, no, other fellow started it." He listened for a minute, then said, "I don't know why. That's my reason for calling. One of the boys has accused Travis of something, I feel silly even bringing it up, but this fellow says Travis and another boy were seen slashing the tires of this fellow's car, in the middle of the night. Yes, the night before last."

After listening for another long period, the principal held the phone against his chest and said to Jerrod, "Travis's father says both of his sons were home all night. When exactly did this incident occur?"

"I don't know, exactly."

"You don't know? So, you didn't actually see it happen?" He put the receiver to his ear again and said, "Hold on a minute, Oliver, I'm trying to get to the bottom of this."

Returning to Jerrod, he asked, "What makes you think it was Travis who slashed your tires?"

"I'd rather not say, sir. It's something that happened the evening before."

"Stop right there, young man. Oliver, forget I called. I don't know what's going on here, but I apologize for bothering you. Right, thanks. My regards to Margaret."

That was the end of it. We were ushered into the hallway and dismissed—Jerrod and I with a stern warning, Travis with a handshake and a pat on the shoulder.

Once outside, I turned on Jerrod. "How could you bring up the tire thing like that? I was on my way out the door with just a slap on the wrist. It was over. And you had to do a dumb thing like that."

"I was mad. Hyatt was kissing Masterson's butt and kicking yours. I saw red." He was quiet for a minute, then said, "You were getting the shaft, man, I could tell. I lost it. Just trying to help you."

"I know," I said, calming down. "I know. I appreciate it. Only thing is, I think we've got bigger problems now than we ever did. 'Stead of letting it drop, you've slapped Travis Masterson in the face with a white glove. Now he'll feel he has to go on with the duel. And you know what?"

"What?"

"We don't know who he's gonna be aiming his pistol at, you or me."

CHAPTER 21

ravis Masterson lost no time letting us know just how much trouble we were in. He was standing in the hallway, not ten feet from Principal Hyatt's door. His feet were planted wide, arms folded across his chest. His brother Tony stood next to him.

Tony was tugging at Travis's sleeve. "C'mon. We don't need this."

Travis shrugged him off, and Tony gave us an embarrassed look. He tried again. "You're going to get into real trouble, Trav. Let's take off. Forget these guys."

"Bug off, little brother. I know what I'm doing. You should've heard old Hyatt on the phone with our big honcho daddy. 'Oh, hello, Oliver. Not a problem, Oliver.' It was choice."

Jerrod and I tried to ignore Travis and slip on by, but he stuck out his foot to trip me. Since it wasn't totally unexpected, I didn't go down, but stumbled awkwardly. I whirled to face Travis, breathing heavily. This was one time when my tendency to stop and think came in handy. Instead of lashing out at Travis and getting myself kicked out of school for sure, I stood and thought of all the possible things I could do.

I decided to smile. "Damn, I'm clumsy," I said. "I sure hope I didn't bruise your toe, stepping on it like that."

Turning my back on Travis, I jabbed Jerrod in the shoulder and said, "I thought you were my friend. You're supposed to stop me from doing stuff like that."

As we walked away, I glanced back at Travis. He hadn't moved, but his arms hung loose and color slowly flooded his face. Tony was behind him, trying hard not to laugh.

At home, Uncle Ty was back from his visit to San Antonio.

"You were wrong about the *señoritas* being tourists from New Jersey," he said. "Mostly they were from California."

"Jeez, Ty. I'm sorry about that. It must have been tough, having to put up with all those surfer girls."

"It was a bitch all right, having to fight them off the whole time. I never made it to the Alamo. Hell, I hardly had time to sleep."

"You were suffering from guilt, because you hadn't taken your favorite nephew along."

"Lordy. Your mother would have killed me. She already thinks I'm a horrible influence on you."

"You are. I'm having impure thoughts all the time."

Ty laughed. "Don't blame that on me, buddy boy. Blame it on hormones."

"Nope. I think I'll keep on blaming it on you. It's a lot more satisfying."

"All right then, glad to be of service."

"Speaking of that," I said, "I could use your advice. But you've got to promise to keep it between us. I don't want Mom to know."

"Okay, shoot."

"Promise?"

"Hey look, kiddo, I can keep a promise. Besides, my sister, who I happen to love, has been through enough in her life. As much as I can, I try to keep from giving her more to worry about. Anyway, I'll soon be outa here. I'm heading home tomorrow. Gotta work for a living every once in a while."

I unloaded everything onto Ty. I told him about the unauthorized trip to the river during the flood, finding and hiding Pedro, and seeing him get into Travis Masterson's truck. I told him about the embarrassing confrontation out on the country bridge and the visit to the principal. Finally, I told him about the discovery of the body in Diablo Creek, a body that I was certain belonged to Pedro.

"What should I do, Ty? Should I tell the police I know who the drowned man is, and where he came from?"

Ty shook his head. "I don't see what good that will do. Besides, guys trying to come into this country illegally drown in the Rio Grande all the time. It's too bad, but there's nothing you and I can do about it."

"But this isn't the Rio Grande. It's right here in Bennington. And he isn't some nameless stranger, he's Pedro, a guy I know. Or knew."

"Sure. But the principle's the same. It jus' taint your problem, little buddy."

My problem with Travis Masterson seemed to be over, too. For the next several days, neither of us said a word as we passed in the hallways. I was beginning to loosen up and relax. Finally, things were back to normal around school—except for the question of Jennifer James. That little issue came to a head on Friday as I turned a corner and just avoided bumping into her. Her expression brightened for a half-second and then settled into a scowl that was chilling on her usually cheerful face.

I stammered, "I'm . . . I'm sorry. But I didn't do it. I swear."

She looked puzzled. "What are you talking about? Of course you did."

"No, I didn't. I swear. Someone else did."

"Peter. You're not making sense. I tried to be friendly the other day, and you took off with some lame excuse about being too busy. I was pretty hurt."

I wanted to say I would never hurt her, that I thought about her all the time, that I'd give anything if the stories were true. Instead I croaked, "I'm talking about the rumors. I'm telling you I didn't start them. I only heard them myself, from Marlene."

"I haven't heard any rumors. I still don't know . . ."

"About *us*. About you and me. I can't imagine what Danny thinks, let alone you."

"Danny?" she said. "Danny Simms? What's he got to do with anything?"

"He and you—you're going together."

"Whoa. Slow down. First of all, Danny and I aren't going together, as you put it. I'm not sure we ever did. We dated for a while, but it was never serious. Second, why should he have any control over who I talk to?"

I felt a hot flush and knew I was blushing again. I looked down at my feet and then back up. "I didn't mean that. It's just . . . oh, hell, I didn't want you to think I read something more into your being nice to me—in the bleachers."

"More than what?"

"More than just being kind to a loser who needed some sympathy and understanding."

"God, you are so dense, Peter. Have you ever stopped to think there may actually have been more?"

"What?"

"My good friend Marlene suffers from diarrhea of the mouth, it seems, but did you ever consider the possibility the rumors she's been spreading might have started with me?"

"You?"

Jennifer threw her hands up in the air and made a complete three-sixty, then covered her eyes and twisted her head while I tried to process all of this data. What she was saying didn't make sense. *She's toying with me, this time for real . . . but no, she's not that kind of person.* I decided she just didn't have any idea about who I was. Who did? Other than Jerrod and Mom's friend, Sarah, no one in the whole state of Texas knew about my past or the mess I was inside.

"You don't even know me," I said, sounding like a frog being strangled.

"I'd like to," she confessed.

My chest felt tight and my throat even more constricted. I could barely push anything through except a feeble, "Lunch?"

Jennifer laughed and ran her finger down my chest. "Lunch then, big boy. It's a date."

She turned away, still chuckling, and skipped off down the hallway, leaving me speechless and red-faced. I looked around to see if anyone had noticed. I hate it when I'm speechless and red-faced. Heading off to English and Mrs. Larson, I was certain the parsing of complex sentences was going to suffer that day. I was going to be too busy making plans for lunch.

When I told Jerrod he'd have to find another date for his mid-day meal, he got this poop-eating grin on his face, but recovered quickly and pretended he was hurt.

"Jilted, I've been jilted. Left standing at the altar. It's mortifying."

"Better to learn what a faithless scoundrel I am now, rather than later."

"I know. I know. Perhaps it's for the best."

"I'm doing you a favor."

"Pete?"

"Yes?"

"When you and Jennifer get hitched, can I be best man?"

I slugged him in the arm, not all that gently, and left to join Jennifer in the food line.

After eating, we moved outside to the concrete tables and benches in the courtyard. Jennifer looked me square in the eyes as I talked. No one had ever looked at me that way. I could see every emotion I was feeling reflected right back at me. I talked and talked. Her light brown hair was cut short, and when she moved her head it bobbed up and down. Her eyes, her hair—I couldn't get enough, and I babbled on and on.

It was almost time to break for our next classes when I realized how I'd monopolized things. I told her it wasn't fair. She was going to have to spill her guts to me, too. We agreed to meet later.

"You sure you'll show this time?"

"Of course."

"You won't wimp out, like last time?"

"Hey, I was operating with an incomplete data set. This time, I'll be there. Guar-an-teed."

After school I raced to the Dairy Queen and arrived out of breath. There was no way Jennifer was going to have to wait for *me*. A quick look inside showed the place was almost empty, so I wandered around outside, scuffing the pavement and examining the leaves on some bushes. Several people walked up from the direction of the school, none of them Jennifer. As time went on, I started to feel this heaviness inside. *She's not coming. She's thought better of it and changed her mind.* When she finally did show, I almost missed her, having convinced myself she wouldn't come. She was almost on top of me when I recognized her bobbing hair, her no-nonsense stride.

"Did I startle you?" she said.

I tried to calm myself, hoping my face wasn't colored to match its warmth. "Just daydreaming, I guess. I do that sometimes."

Inside, we each ordered a shake, and I insisted on buying. I was relieved to find I had enough money in my pocket to cover it. We sat in a booth away from the door and continued our conversation. This time she did most of the talking. I looked her square in the face like she'd watched me earlier, anxious to demonstrate my interest. I was soon lost in her story and forgot to worry about how I appeared.

She'd lived in Bennington her whole life. Her parents were divorced and both remarried. Luckily, neither had moved out of town so it was easy enough to spend time with both of them. She liked her stepfather and tolerated her stepmother.

"She's all right, I guess. I wasn't easy on her at first, and she resented it. We're still not close, but at least we both understand why the other acts the way she does."

"I can't imagine having four parents," I said. "For half my life I've only had one."

She nodded her head, offering me a closed-lip smile of sympathy. I felt another surge of warmth.

"You said at lunch you had a lot on your mind. Anything you want to talk about?"

I thought for a minute. The business with Pedro was a secret between me and Jerrod. Did I have the right to spill it to someone else? Of course it was me, not Jerrod, who had insisted on keeping it a secret.

I decided to plunge in and told her the whole story.

"... and I'm pretty torn up about it. To rescue a guy, get to know him, and then he goes back and gets himself drowned anyway."

Jennifer narrowed her eyes and tilted her head slightly. "You didn't read this morning's paper, I guess."

"Nope, not yet."

"Then you wouldn't know. The coroner's report was released yesterday. It said the guy who was found in Diablo Creek didn't drown. He was dead before he went into the water, killed by a blow to the head."

"You mean he hit it on a rock?"

"They don't think so. There were rope marks and bruises all over his body. They're saying it wasn't an accident. Your friend Pedro was murdered."

CHAPTER 22

Oh, Dad!

Some pretty heavy stuff is going down around here, and I don't know whether I'm sitting right in the middle of it or just a bystander looking in from ringside.

That Hispanic guy we fished out of the river took off. We figured he went back to wherever he was working because his younger brother and sister were still there. He had to go back, see, even though he was afraid of the place for some reason. Anyway, Pedro—that's his name—shows up in the river again. This time he's really dead. Worse, it looks for sure like he was murdered. Can you believe?

I wonder what you would do under these circumstances. For some strange reason, teaching me what to do when someone I know turns up dead wasn't one of life's little lessons you taught me, Dad. At least not in words. I guess you figured a hands-on demonstration would be more effective, right?

Sorry, I keep getting sidetracked. As I was saying, I find out Pedro's been murdered from Jennifer. She read it in the paper. We're sitting in the Dairy Queen, and she springs this on me while I'm sucking up a chocolate milkshake.

CHAPTER 28

eter? You've gone all pale. Do you need some water or something? I'm so sorry about Pedro."

I waved Jennifer off to let her know I needed time to think. I closed my eyes.

"I've got to find Jerrod. We need to talk."

"He's right over there. He came in ten minutes ago, but I guess he didn't want to interrupt."

"Why didn't you tell me?"

"Because I wanted you to myself for a little while. Was that so terrible?"

"No. I wanted to be alone with you, too, and I'd have felt, you know, obligated to invite him over. But now . . ."

"I'll leave you guys alone." Jennifer got up. "Thanks for the shake, Peter. When you've done whatever it is you have to do, let me know." She trailed one finger across the top my hand. "Please be careful."

I felt a strange sense of dread as I watched Jennifer walk away. It was like everything good in life was leaving and I was about to enter a new and frightening world. I was caught up in events I couldn't escape. I walked slowly toward Jerrod, already certain that "be careful" was destined to be futile advice.

Jerrod and I argued immediately about our next step. He now wanted to go to the police and tell them everything. I thought it would be useless, at best. The minute we said something to incriminate Travis, they'd learn all about the fight at school and what happened in the principal's office.

"With Principal Hyatt and that a-hole Petit against me, it will look like we're only making trouble. And with Travis's dad being such a big shot in town, well you know how it'll go. Travis'll get a pat on the head, and you and I'll get shafted."

"We've gotta tell someone."

"It won't do any good. You know this town better than me. No one will believe us, and it won't bring Pedro back."

Jerrod didn't say anything for a minute, then nodded.

"You're right. Pedro's dead. It's finished."

I felt a rush of adrenaline at a sudden thought. I gripped the edge of the table.

"What's the matter, Pete?"

"It isn't finished, and we can't forget it. Pedro was tied up and beaten before he was killed. What about Juan and Carlina? If they're still alive, maybe they're being knocked around, tortured, raped."

"Hell. Okay, so we tell someone. Some adult. How about your Uncle Tyler?"

I shook my head. "Afraid not. He left a couple of days ago."

"So what do we do? What master Einsteinian plan are you gonna spring on us now?"

I didn't say anything for a long time. There are times when I blunder into things without realizing it, as hard as I try to avoid anything that gives a hint of trouble. There are other, rare times when I know what I'm about to say is going to send life spinning off in a new direction. It was like some stranger had taken over my body and was planning things that cautious, careful Pete Grayson never would.

I stared at the ceiling, then challenged Jerrod. "I think we should follow Travis again."

"What? Are you some kind of idiot? Remember last time, we almost got the stuffing kicked out of us? Jeez, Pete. I ended up with four shredded tires."

"We'll be more careful."

"You're a jerk, Grayson." Jerrod laid his head on the table. When he looked up, he said, "And I'm even more of a jerk for going along with you."

I gave him a fist to knock, but he slapped it away.

The plan was to follow Masterson's truck each day after school to see if he went anywhere other than home. We needed to find out where he took Pedro after picking him up in the alley. Most importantly, we needed proof we could take to the authorities that evil things were happening in our quiet little town.

To keep from being spotted again, we decided to call it quits any time we had to get too close to the pickup. It promised to be a long process, unless we caught a break right off the bat. We didn't. Every day for a week we eased into traffic as far behind Travis as we could. Sometimes he had Heather Barnes or one of the other Bennington Bimbos with him. Most of the time, his brother Tony rode with him. They generally tooled around town for a while, honking at friends. Stopped at intersections, Travis raced his engine, daring other cars to race. He seemed to get special pleasure challenging Bennington's senior citizens, several of whom waved a clenched fist out the window as the gray pickup roared off. Travis always returned the greeting with a one-finger salute.

When they finally went home, it was to a big ranch-style house on the outskirts of town, with a lawn that looked like it was weeded with tweezers or something. Through square-clipped hedges, we caught a glimpse of this Mediterranean-colored swimming pool. When the pickup neared the house, we made a U-turn and gave it up.

Twice, Travis left school with Bulldog Brandon instead of Tony. They stopped for a hamburger both times, then went to Brandon's place. This was our cue to break it off, too. There was no way we were going try to hide behind that piddly screen of trees like last time.

On Friday, with the sky overcast and ominous, we made our brilliant move. When Travis and Bulldog stopped at the Brandon house, we waited until they were inside and then drove straight past and out the country road where we'd gotten into trouble the first time. We figured if our prey stuck to the same habits, they might drive the same way. If they didn't see anyone behind them as they left Bulldog's, then they might not notice picking up a tail later. Like I said, brilliant.

There's an old saying that goes, "Be careful what you wish for. You just might get it." This might have been written about the Friday afternoon we crossed the Diablo Creek bridge, looking for a good place to hide.

Our part of Texas is made up mostly of farmland and cow pastures. There are few places where trees and bushes have been left standing and none that also include a spot where we could hide a car and still see the road. The best we could come up with was an abandoned building, a decrepit old Swiss cheese of a barn, more holes than cheese. It was just beyond the Diablo Creek bridge and off the road on the right.

There was still no escaping the fact Jerrod's car was *red*. Earlier, I'd very cleverly anticipated this problem by grabbing an old paint-spattered tarp out of Jerrod's garden shed.

"Here, stick this in the back seat," I'd told Jerrod.

"I've always wondered about you. Now I know you've gone completely off your gourd. What do you plan on painting?"

"It's the paint that's already on your car I'm worried about."

When we parked behind the old barn, we spread the tarp out and covered Jerrod's car so no flash of red would catch Travis's eye. The wind had picked up, and we had to weight the tarp down with rocks from a crumbling old wall. Every once in a while I felt a drop of rain. Beyond the barn, there was a steep incline down to the creek. To our left, directly away from the road, the land sloped more gently down to where the creek meandered in a lazy loop. In the late afternoon light, I could make out the reflection of orange sky bouncing off the water.

While we waited, we decided to explore the old barn. It was pretty grotty. The main door had fallen or blown off in some windstorm long ago, so it was easy to get in. The long sides were pretty much intact, but the ends of the barn were leaning inward at a dangerous angle because the main roof beam had rotted and fallen to the floor. The whole structure was shaking in the wind, and it creaked when it was hit with a sudden gust.

"Stay in the middle," I warned.

"Not to worry. I wouldn't go near those walls if my life depended on it."

"It might. Could be snakes or rabid opossums or armadillos under all that junk."

I was using a long stick to lift up a board, trying not to freak at a mess of field mice scurrying out, and discovered a hinged square of wood in the floor. With a small stick, I pried under the door and we lifted it up.

I said, "Some sort of cellar, I suppose. In Connecticut, the really old houses had root cellars."

I didn't think this cellar was full of vegetables. Looking down into the blackness, I shuddered to think what might actually be lurking down there. We let the door crash down when we heard a car coming. Running outside, we craned our necks around the side of the building. It was just an old farm truck, but less than a minute later we caught the sound of another vehicle and the glint of gray paint. Masterson's pickup.

As soon as they whizzed by, I crumpled up the tarp and stuffed it into the back seat while Jerrod started the car. We tore off after Travis, afraid we'd lost him. We were on a farm road that every once in a while made right-angle turns, following property boundaries. When we came to a T-junction, there was no way of knowing whether Travis had turned right or left. Guessing, we turned left, and soon I was relieved to see a flash of metallic gray through some trees. Travis had left the road and was heading toward a group of low buildings off in the distance.

"Now what, Pete?" said Jerrod. "We can't follow him in, but there's nowhere to park out here."

"Go on by the driveway entrance."

"There's still nowhere to hide a car."

"We don't have to. We can park right alongside the road if we go far enough ahead. There's not much chance they'll drive *away* from town."

"Oh, yeah, right."

We parked and hiked directly across the field, keeping a hedge of bushes between us and the gravel driveway. I guessed the buildings were about a quarter-mile from the road, maybe a bit more. By the time we got close, our shoes were heavy with mud, a dark adobe that grabbed on and wouldn't let go. We sat behind a clump of bushes and tried to peel the mucky clay off as best we could. It was getting so we could scarcely walk, and I was afraid we'd have to do a lot more than walk before we found out what Travis and Bulldog were up to. Somewhere beyond the layer of dull clouds, the sun was setting. The clouds were thickening, so it was suddenly really dark. As we sat in the bushes, it started to pour.

"Oh, hell. We're gonna get soaked," said Jerrod.

"Look on the bright side, man. They'll probably stay inside, and we'll be able to look around easier."

"If I can't get this muck off my shoes, it's not going to be any easier."

"Just lay on your back with your feet in the air. The rain'll wash 'em clean."

"Doofus."

"Quit whining."

Crawling through the wet bushes, we were instantly soaked. The rain couldn't possibly make us any wetter.

There were three wooden buildings, all low and flat-roofed. On the right, two were connected by a covered walkway, the sides of which had been boarded up to form a kind of tunnel. The third building, the largest, stood alone on the left. None of them had a door on the side facing us. No lights showed in any of the buildings, but then, we couldn't see any windows, either. *This is good. They can't see us.* But then we couldn't see inside either, so what was the point in being there?

There were two cars parked to the right of the buildings. One was Travis's pickup; the other was a maroon SUV. Jerrod and I decided our first move would be to circle around to the back and see if there were any more cars parked out of our line of sight and if there were windows on the far side. Since there wasn't any visible cover in back, Jerrod motioned to me to follow him up to the front of the center building. We crept along the left side to the back. Jerrod squatted down, I leaned over him, and we both peered around the corner. Nothing. No cars, no lights.

Cautiously, we moved out so we could see the back sides of the two connected buildings. The one furthest from us had a door and one window showing a thin crack of light around the edges of dark blinds. The one nearest us had no openings of any kind.

"You must have to go through the tunnel to get into this one," I whispered.

"What about the big building behind us? See anything?"

"All dark. No windows on this side either. One door."

"Guess everyone's in Building One where the light is. What do we do now? Sit here in the rain until someone comes out?"

"I suppose we wait for a while. There are bushes over there."

A line of yellow light suddenly appeared on the ground in front of the door. It widened into a rectangle filled with the shadow of someone bursting through the opening. I dropped to the ground in a panic, and Jerrod fell on top of me. It took a minute to realize the people in front of us were way too busy to notice a couple of kids cowering in the half-darkness.

Two people were running toward the field. The one who'd fled through the door first was small and thin, with flowing hair. A girl? I knew for sure, when she screamed. Her pursuer, a large, muscular man, caught up with her and straight-armed her in the back, throwing her to the ground. She continued to scream as the man pulled her to her feet by her hair and slapped her repeatedly. As the guy shoved the sobbing girl back toward the building, another man exploded through the doorway, waving his arms wildly and shouting.

"¡No! Salga ella solo. Cerdo!"

This second man was short and rail-thin. For a brief moment I thought it was Pedro, until I remembered Pedro was dead, *murdered*, and very possibly by the same man standing not forty feet away from me. I was certain of two things. First, these were Pedro's brother and sister, Juan and Carlina. The second was I was scared out of my gourd, and had only myself to blame for being there.

The one I took to be Juan ran forward, waving his arms wildly. The big man grabbed the girl by the hair again and threw her to the ground. He stood stock-still and then, with a move so quick I could barely see it, he flattened Juan with a single blow to the head. He stepped forward and drew his foot back to kick the inert form on the ground, then changed his mind. Instead, he drew a gun out of his waistband and placed it against the small man's forehead.

"Do you know how lucky you are, *amigo*? Do you?" His voice was deep and grated like sandpaper. "I'd very much like to kill you, you know that? I'd love to run my size eleven Justin's into your head so many times your brain'd be scattered half-way to Mexico. Lucky for you, with your trouble-making brother gone, the boss needs you more'n he did before."

He spun Juan over with a hard shove of his foot. "But don't forget there's a million more like you where you come from. You and the *señorita* give me one more lick of trouble, another trip across the border wouldn't be no *problema* at all. *Comprende?"*

By then the girl had crawled over and was crying out, "Juanito. Ay, Juanito."

"Get her back inside," the big man commanded. Only then did I realize someone else was standing in the doorway. It was Travis Masterson, with Bulldog Brandon right behind him.

Seizing the girl by the shoulders and marching her toward the door, Travis said, "Smarten up, Carlina. Do what Mr. Dyer says. Don't forget . . . don't forget what happened to Pedro."

At his words, Carlina howled really loud, and Travis pushed her into the arms of Bulldog, who hustled her inside. Travis and the man named Dyer grabbed Juan under the arms and dragged him into the building. Slowly the rectangle of yellow light narrowed to a thin line and was gone.

Jerrod and I were lying prone in the mud. For the longest time I couldn't move. There were no bones in my legs and I was shaking. I realized I'd been holding my breath, and I gulped in deep lungfuls of air. When I could stand, I staggered into the darkness between the buildings and Jerrod followed. Neither of us said a word. When we got back to the shelter of our clump of bushes in front, we collapsed again.

"I've seen enough," I said. "I have no clue what's going on here, but whatever it is, Pedro's brother and sister are being held against their will."

"At least that Dyer dude said he wouldn't kill them 'cause the 'boss' needs them," Jerrod pointed out hopefully.

"I wouldn't count on it staying that way. I suspect they needed Pedro, too."

"Let's get out of here, Pete."

"No argument from me."

"Hold on. I hear someone."

Creeping back through the soggy bushes, we saw several people walking toward the cars in the dull light angling out of the doorway. Two of them were talking.

". . . kill us if this shipment gets ruined. It's still raining."

"Not a chance. It's double-wrapped in plastic. It'll be fine."

"It sure as hell better be. If it gets wet, it'll be my butt, not yours. Your daddy would never blame you, Daddy's pride and joy."

Travis drew his arm back, but Bulldog grabbed it and pulled him away. "Cool it, Trav. Not worth the hassle."

"You got that right, Dog," said Dyer, his hand poised menacingly over the butt of his gun. "Now, let's get this stuff loaded and you out of here. We've wasted enough time, what with our *pachuco* and his little sister giving us fits." He shook his head. "I knew it was a mistake bringin' these kids here. Why couldn't we have found good ol' Americans to work the damn lab?"

Bulldog and Travis loaded half-a-dozen blue, plastic-wrapped boxes into the back of the pickup while Jerrod and I continued to hover in our rain-soaked hiding place. Despite the muggy warmth of the evening, I started shivering. As soon as they'd finished, Bulldog hopped into the passenger seat. Before Travis climbed in to drive, he called out, "Think you can handle your little girl without our help, Dyer?"

I couldn't hear the reply, but Travis jumped into the pickup, laughing the same chilling laugh we'd heard that night on the bridge. As the gray pickup circled around the building to the driveway, its headlights swept across the thicket where Jerrod and I were hiding. We ducked down and laid with our cheeks pressed into the mud. Had they spotted us? It seemed like the truck had hesitated a bit before accelerating down the drive. We didn't relax until the taillights had disappeared into the darkness as the pickup turned onto the road.

Our relief was short-lived. The pickup reversed and turned again. The red of the taillights was replaced by the piercing gleam of headlights. Travis Masterson was on his way back, and he was moving fast.

CHAPTER 24

Our only hope was that Travis was returning because he'd forgotten something, not because he'd seen us. He roared past us to the back of the building, leaped out of the truck, and disappeared. We could barely make out the faint glow of light from the door opening and closing.

"Should we make a break for it?" asked Jerrod.

"Man, I don't think so. I'd hate to get caught in the open field."

Sure enough, Travis quickly came back out, jumped into the truck, and peeled off down the driveway.

"Jeez, I was scared," said Jerrod. "I thought he'd spotted us."

"Me, too. He slowed down the first time he went by, like maybe he'd seen something."

We waited until Travis had reached the road again, and then Jerrod said, "Okay. Let's go. Now!"

We raced up the driveway, instead of cutting over through the field to the row of bushes we'd used before. This time we wanted speed. We needed to get the hell out of there, the quicker the better.

"Oh, no . . ."

"Damn."

Travis was turning around again. He was going to head back down the driveway and catch us like two startled deer. I turned so fast I slipped in the mud and fell. Jerrod stopped to help me up and we sprinted like crazy, diving head-first into our old hiding place. My face stung from the grasping branches, and I tasted blood from a cut on my lip. I tried to make myself small, to disappear into the ground.

Jerrod was shaking, whimpering in short, little gasps. I might have been, too; I could hear almost nothing over the pounding in my chest. Every breath was painful. I put my hand on Jerrod's arm, hoping the touch might calm us both. He put his hand on top of mine and held it. We waited, breathless, as the gray pickup sped toward us. My mind was reeling with possibilities, switching between hope and fear. *He's seen us. No, he's forgotten something else. No, he saw something but doesn't know what it is. No, if he'd seen us why did he go back to the road?*

The answer came soon enough. Travis slammed on the brakes and skidded to a stop with his headlights pointed directly at our hiding place. He was less than twenty feet away. We squashed ourselves down even further, but I knew it was no use. We'd had it, for sure. I heard both car doors open and knew Travis and Bulldog would be on us in about two seconds.

"Run!" I shouted at Jerrod, clambering through the shrubbery. I barely felt the stinging slaps of branches and thorns. Reaching the far side, away from Travis and the accusing headlights, I scrambled to my feet, Jerrod right behind me. When I stopped, Jerrod crashed into me. He said, "Wha . . ." before realizing what had caused me to freeze.

In front of us, half in shadow and half lit by the headlights' glare, stood the man called Dyer. His eyes were like black holes in a whitewashed face—a face contorted in a lopsided grin that told me he was going to greatly enjoy whatever was coming next. It wasn't Dyer or his grin that chilled me the most, though. It was the cold flash of metal pointed directly at my chest.

"My, my," he said. "What do we have here? Two little peckernuts caught in the bushes."

Travis and Bulldog ran up then. Bulldog snarled, "I shoulda known who it was."

Travis said, "What is it with you? Hard to believe you guys are this dumb. What's your story this time? Just following someone at random. Just happened to be us—again?"

"Who the hell are these two clowns?" asked Dyer. "You know them?"

"Yeah. We know 'em," said Travis. "They've been nothing but trouble for weeks. Thing is, I can't figure out why. I beat the crap out of old Airball here. Why he seems to want more of the same— well, who knows?"

"Let's get inside." Dyer's voice was menacing—gravelly and breathy, like he was speaking through a gas mask. "C'mon, Dog, you and me get these two in where I can get a good look-see at 'em. Travis, bring the truck on back."

We staggered through the mud toward the rear of the building. I tripped several times. It was impossible to think about my feet because I was thinking about my back, the spot in my back where Dyer's gun was pointed. I imagined the sting of the bullet. Or would it feel like a two-by-four slammed into me? I didn't know. Would I go unconscious right off, or would I lay there feeling my life's blood running out onto the ground and thinking of all the things I wanted to do that I hadn't yet?

I stumbled across the threshold and into the brightly lit room. Slowly my eyes adjusted to the glare. Jerrod lay on the concrete floor where he'd fallen after Bulldog shouldered him through the door.

The room was about ten feet wide and twice as long. One end was fixed up as an office, with a desk, a bookcase, and a small free-standing safe. The far end of the room looked more like a living room. There was a couch, a couple of faded green upholstered chairs, two battered side-tables with lamps. Another bookcase was filled with paperbacks. An old-fashioned wooden clock sat on top.

Dyer pressed the gun into the side of my face and growled, "Now, I want y'all to feel right at home here. Understand? Why don'tcha grab a seat on the couch yonder and make yourselves comfy?"

I was only too happy to go along with this if it would remove the pressure of cold steel from my temple. My mind flashed back to my father, lying in a pool of blood, with parts of his head sprayed all over the room. It was an image I'd been trying to erase from my mind for eight years. I threw myself onto the couch and sat with my back straight, feet planted on the floor, and hands held together in my lap. I realized Jerrod had leaned back and crossed his legs. *He's scared, but he's trying hard to look cool and all.* I put my hands behind my head, linking fingers, and crossed my own legs. *If Jerrod can do it . . .*

Travis and Bulldog leaned against the wall. They were fidgety and looked uncomfortable. That concerned me. I figured if those two tough guys were nervous, they must have some idea of what was in store for us, and it wasn't going to be pleasant. I glanced at Jerrod; he gave me a quick smile, then stretched and let out a huge yawn. I started to do the same but realized it would seem just *too* bogus. I tried to listen as Dyer talked to someone on the telephone.

". . . sure, I understand. Yeah, the boys know 'em, who they are. Couple of kids from school. No, no idea . . . . Right. We're not going anywhere, and neither are they."

Dyer hung up the phone and stared at a blank wall for a minute. Then he nodded his head a couple of times, grabbed the desk chair, and slammed it down in front of us. Sitting backwards on the chair, he leaned into it and fixed his eyes first on Jerrod, then me. His pupils were dark and intense.

Still looking at us, he spoke to Travis. "Your dad'll be here soon's he can. In the meantime, we wait."

Travis asked, "What did he say we were going to do?"

Dyer didn't answer. I was finding it harder and harder to act cool. Jerrod, I could see out of the corner of my eye, was rocking back and forth. I knew he was coming to the same bitter realization I was; we were imprisoned by the people who had killed Pedro. Dyer had shown, with every evil word and gesture, he'd have a great old time killing two more.

I wanted to curl up on the couch in a ball, but I decided to talk. I figured if I kept making noise, I could maybe tough things out.

"What is this place? Some kind of farm?"

Travis and Bulldog looked at each other. Dyer spoke up. "Not your business, kid. Never was. You were stupid to come here."

"How could we know it was stupid if we didn't know anything about it?"

Travis said, "Now *that's* stupid. You dumb asses follow us out here. Then what do you do? Do you walk up to the door and say, 'Hey, we were in the neighborhood—thought we'd drop in'? No, you hide in the frigging bushes. You knew damn well it was stupid." He spun away and leaned into the desk with both hands.

"So we're not too smart," said Jerrod. "That's not a crime is it?"

Travis shook his head, then turned back to us. "I have no problem figuring you for a dorkbrain, Jerrod. But Airball here, I don't think so. There's more to it than you guys are saying."

"We haven't said nuthin."

"Oh, you will." Dyer stood.

He opened the door to the passageway leading to the other building and went through, closing it quickly behind him. For the brief second the door was open, I heard the low sound of voices. *Too late. We already know who's down there.* It didn't seem like a good idea, though, to let our captors know what we knew. Especially about Pedro. I only hoped Jerrod realized the same thing and didn't go blabbing his mouth off. When Dyer came back, I listened for any sound of Juan and Carlina, but this time it was quiet down the hallway.

Oliver Masterson arrived in less than half an hour. He must have had his foot to the floorboard. *He feels we're important enough to drop everything and barrel out here. Another bad sign.*

He strode into the room, glanced at Jerrod and me, then spoke to Dyer, who seemed to shrink and lose all his blustery authority the minute his boss came into the room.

"Bill, outside. Travis, you, too. Bulldog, watch these two."

Masterson turned on his heel and marched out, Travis and Dyer following quickly. A big, powerfully built man, Oliver Masterson was obviously used to giving orders, and to having people obey him. Everyone, including the vicious Bill Dyer, danced when he pulled the strings.

When the others left, Brandon started marching around, all puffed up, issuing his own orders—stand, sit, talk, be quiet. Everything he said was in a breaking voice, and I could tell he was really hyper about whatever was going down.

"So how bad of trouble are we in?" I asked him.

"How should I know? I just work here. Usually not even that. I just bring stuff in and out with Trav."

"What kind of stuff?"

"Forget it. You don't wanta know."

"What's gonna happen to us?"

"That you *really* don't want to know."

Jerrod leaned forward, holding his head. His last shred of cool was gone. I felt a heaviness in my chest and a pounding in my temples. It took all of my strength to sit upright and try to look super cool. Jerrod had succumbed to his terror; it was up to me to stay in control.

When they came back inside, Oliver Masterson looked serious, Bill Dyer was grinning like he'd just won the lottery, and Travis picked nervously at his shirt sleeve. I imagined a jury about to give someone the death penalty might look like Travis.

Oliver Masterson started to speak, but before he could get any-thing out, the door opened a crack and someone stuck his head in. "Hey, what's going on?"

Oliver whirled. "Tony! I told you to stay in the damn car."

"I don't understand why. I saw Travis's pickup. Why can't I . . ."

"Because I told you to! This isn't your business. Damn it, Tony, I wanted to keep you out of this."

Tony pushed open the door and came all the way in. "If it's family business, I . . ." He stared at each of us in turn.

"Bulldog? Jerrod? Peter? What the . . ."

"Just shut up, Tony, and let me think," said Masterson. "What a mess. First these idiots, and now you."

He paced. Whenever anyone started to speak, he'd shut them off with a violent wave of his hand and a dark scowl. I sat on the edge of the couch, watching him, all thought of keeping cool gone.

When he stopped, Masterson took a deep breath and then spoke to his younger son.

"We don't have much of a choice. This wasn't your business, Tony, but you refused to obey me and keep your nose out of it and your butt in the car. So now you're part of it, too, like it or not."

"Part of what?"

Masterson looked over at us, then back at Tony. "Later. I'll explain it to you later. Right now, I've got to figure out what to do with these punks."

Dyer spoke up. "I say we . . ."

"Later, Bill. We talk later. Perhaps I didn't make myself clear."

Dyer and everyone else got quiet. All I could hear was the tick of the clock, and I swear my heart started to pump in sync with it. In the silence, the clock took over the room.

"Make us part of it," I improvised.

"What was that?" said Masterson.

"We're here 'cause we need work. A couple of American boys that need work." I checked Dyer to see if he'd caught what I was saying. He frowned and tilted his head to one side.

"What makes you think you're qualified to work here?" Oliver Masterson smiled. He seemed to find my request amusing.

"What could be so hard about it?"

I didn't have a clue what they did, but I figured if the three Nicaraguans could do it, so could Jerrod and me. There was no way I could let on I knew about the Nicaraguans, though.

Travis said, "But you just told us you didn't . . ."

"Shut up, Travis," his father said. Travis wilted. I almost felt sorry for him, being under this tyrant's thumb.

"Good try, young man, but I don't think I can trust you."

"Bring us in on it, and we'll be part of it." I was still bluffing, trying to talk us out of whatever trouble we were in.

Masterson narrowed his eyes. "So what skills do you bring to our little business?"

I stammered, "Things like, uh, well . . ."

"Put them in the lab," said Masterson, abruptly. "It's secure. It'll give us time to figure out what to do with them."

Dyer jumped up, his demented glee back in full force. "Off you go, little dogies, it's roundup time."

He jerked me to my feet, then reached for Jerrod. Jerrod pressed back into the couch, and Dyer grabbed a handful of hair and yanked him forward. When Jerrod squealed, Dyer laughed and pulled harder. Jerrod had no choice but to stand. When Dyer let loose of him, he didn't move. He stood sullenly.

Travis and Dyer propelled us roughly through the door and across the muddy ground to the far building that stood alone. We passed directly over the spot where Jerrod and I had lain earlier, pressed into the mud, watching Carlina being caught and dragged by a cursing Bill Dyer. Dyer pulled out a fat bundle of keys and chose one, which he used to turn a deadbolt in the door. He used another key to release a second lock before the door swung open. It was made of heavy metal and set in a metal frame. Its hinges were solid and well-oiled; the door swung open without a sound.

Dyer shoved me through. I tripped on the doorjamb and stumbled into the room, ending up chin-first on the concrete floor. Jerrod crashed into my back. Both locks were turned again. I lay in the dark for a long time, afraid to move, afraid to discover something was broken.

"You okay, Jerrod?"

"How okay could I be?" He was still beside me on the floor.

"I mean, is anything broken?"

"I don't think so."

"Me neither. Jeez, it's dark."

"If you remember," said Jerrod, "this building didn't have any windows, not that they'd do any good on a dark night in a rain storm."

"I'll try to find a light switch." I crawled backwards to where I thought the door was, but bumped into some kind of table leg. Moving left, I was able to grope back several more feet before I hit the wall. Feeling with my fingertips, I found what seemed to be the door. I stood up and searched each side for a light switch. Nothing.

"We need to check this place out. Come stand next to me."

Jerrod crawled toward me, guided by my voice, and I helped him stand.

"Okay. You go right and I'll go left. We'll feel our way around the room. When you recognize something, call it out, so we both know what we're into. The first thing you're going to bump into is something with a leg, maybe a bench."

"Maybe Frankenstein's monster. It had a leg—or two."

I was glad to hear Jerrod's sense of humor hadn't been completely frightened out of him. It gave me hope, though there was very little we could hope for.

Going left, I hit something solid right off and decided it was definitely a high bench, topped with plywood.

"Got a workbench," Jerrod said just then.

"Me, too. I'm scared to feel around on top of it without light, if this really is some kind of a lab. Let's just keep moving and check out the big stuff first, before we worry about what's on top."

"Workbench . . . workbench . . . workbench."

"Workbench . . . workbench . . . *end* of workbench. I can feel the bare wall here. Now something else, like a desk or a . . . yes!"

"What, Pete?"

"Electrical cord, plugged into an outlet. I'm following it along. Bingo, it's a lamp."

Fumbling along the base of the lamp and up toward the bulb, I found a switch. The light, when it came on, was blinding.

"You did it, Pete. Excellent!" Jerrod hurried over and pounded on my shoulder.

I turned around and tried to take in the room all at once, saving the details for after my eyes adjusted. There were workbenches on three sides and part of the fourth. In the open space was a small desk where the lamp stood. Fluorescent light fixtures were hanging from the ceiling over the workbenches. The electricity that supplied them traveled through conduit strapped to the ceiling and down the wall near the door. I would have run into the switch if I'd only searched a foot or two further away from the door.

Jerrod moved to turn on the main lights.

"Wait," I said. "I don't think there are any cracks where they could see bright light, but you never know. Let's use just the lamp for now. No sense alerting Masterson and crew."

"Oh, yeah. Keep them sweet and good-natured, huh?"

"This is definitely a lab."

"For what?"

"I don't think they're making perfume, numbnuts. Some sort of narcotics, probably. What else?"

"What do you think they're going to do with us, Pete?"

"As I see it, they've got three choices. They can turn themselves in to the cops—that seems like a long-shot to me."

"And?"

"They can close up shop, pack up their lab and their business, and move it somewhere else."

"You think?"

"Oliver Masterson is a big shot in Bennington. He's got a wife and kids and probably has cocktails with the mayor. What do you think?"

"I guess no. So, what's their third choice?"

"I think, like Bulldog said, we don't really want to know."

CHAPTER 25

Jerrod stared at me for several long seconds. Fear gave way to anger.

"They can't get away with this. It's off-the-wall crazy. Stuff like this doesn't happen in Bennington, Texas."

"A week ago, I'd have agreed with you. But here we are. And remember Pedro."

"Oh, man."

"Pedro happened."

"I know. Man, we've got to get out of here!"

"Sounds like a good idea, but I'll bet this building is built like a fortress, considering what they do here."

"So what *do* they do?"

I checked out the counter tops. "Let's see. There's bottles of chemicals and stuff, beakers and test tubes. Distillation columns, maybe. Two-gallon jars that say Acetone. One that says Alcohol. A couple of Bunsen burners. I think maybe these big things are ovens."

"Here's some trays of something drying that looks like clear hard candy. What do you think, crack maybe?"

"Or ice," I said. Jerrod looked puzzled so I said, "Speed, made so it can be smoked. Hits like a freight train. Coming down is just as fast. You feel like you've been nailed by a ton of bricks. I knew a guy in Connecticut who tried it only once. He went crazy trying to find another hit. People get addicted just like that—wham, bang. Nasty stuff."

"This is big time, Pete. These clowns have got a lot to lose, don't they?"

"Enough so's I think they're gonna be pretty damn desperate. Much as I can't stand Travis and Bulldog, I don't think they're anything like murderers—but that guy Dyer is a nasty one. I think he enjoys hurting people. It's good to see him squirm when old Masterson bosses him around, but . . ."

"That still doesn't tell me what they're gonna do."

"What I'm afraid of is they've got themselves backed into a corner."

"Which means?"

"It means they're going to have to get rid of us."

Jerrod stared at me. His face fell; any shred of hope he might have had was now gone.

"Pete?"

"What?"

"I'm scared."

"Me, too." I took a deep breath. " But we can't just stand here and be scared. We gotta get ourselves out of here."

"How?"

"Look for tools. Saws, hammers, knives, anything that might help us."

We each started pulling out drawers and looking through cupboards. I found one almost full of boxes with small plastic packets of the dried narcotic, broken into small pieces. I finally found tools in some drawers under one of the workbenches. They weren't much— several screwdrivers of various sizes, pliers, and a hacksaw. Then in the back, I found something much more promising, an electric drill and a set of high-speed drill bits.

Jerrod said, "Good going, Einstein. Let's bust the locks off this joint and split."

"You sound like Al Capone. There's two problems with that plan—make it three. First, we'd probably have to drill for a week before we could tear up two deadbolts enough to get them open. Second, they'd hear us for sure drilling on that metal door."

"Okay, okay. You win, already. But I know you want to tell me what the third problem is."

"The third problem is—we couldn't drill it anyway. The door's over there, the electrical outlet's over here, and we don't have an extension cord."

To make use of the drill, it would have to be done close to the outlet. Also, someone might check on us, so we needed to hide our escape preparations until we were ready to actually leave. The answer seemed pretty obvious, shove the desk aside and try to make a hole in the wall behind it. If someone came, we could shove the desk back, and they wouldn't know what we were up to. Maybe.

"Like those movies where they tunnel out of Nazi prison camps and hide the entrance under the stove or something."

I was pretty sure the outside of the building was made of wood. The inside was solid wood, so I figured we'd have to break through two tough layers at least. Behind the desk I used the largest drill bit to make two holes close to each other and then tilted the drill back and forth until they joined together in a little slot.

"Now what?" said Jerrod. "I don't think I can squeeze through that."

Good. Jerrod was still able to joke. That meant he could still keep going without curling up in a ball, like I felt I wanted to do.

"I told you to go easy on the pizza. Can you get the hacksaw blade out of its frame without breaking it?"

I found an old rag and wrapped it around the blade so I could hold it without tearing up my hand. Slipping it into the slot, I cut down about six inches. Jerrod did the same, sideways. Then I took over again and cut on the diagonal. It was slow going, but when a triangle of wood fell away, we both whooped. We could see through to the siding on the outside.

"That was the hard part. Now there's room to put the hacksaw blade back in its frame, and we can cut a lot faster."

Sure enough, it was fairly easy to keep cutting away triangles until we had a hole big enough for us to fit through. We started the same thing on the outer wall, grateful it was on the side of the lab away from the other buildings. The outside paneling was made of softer wood. It was looking good. As the first triangle fell away, we felt the cool, moist air of freedom.

A key turned in the lock. I jumped to my feet like a scalded cat and helped Jerrod push the desk back into place. As the second lock was being turned, we ran to the other side of the room and sat on a couple of lab stools. The door swung open and Bill Dyer walked in.

"Hello, girls. What have you been up to?"

"Nothing," said Jerrod.

"You were making an awful lot of noise for nothing."

Why didn't we think of some way to account for noise?

"We were trying to escape," I said, sneering.

Jerrod looked at me like I'd gone crazy, but I ignored him and kept talking to Dyer. I reached into my pocket and pulled out a quarter.

"I was using this quarter to scrape a hole through the wall. But the wood's too hard. It wasn't working."

Dyer laughed. "Well, kid, stupid idea, but I gotta give you credit for trying. It might've worked—in about a hundred years. Unfortunately for you, you don't have a hundred years." He paused. "You also don't have a quarter."

He grabbed it out of my hand. I put on a sad face to hide how clever I was feeling inside. Even better than that, I felt *fast*. Instead of making up a list of all the possible things to do, I'd just grabbed the first one that came to mind and went with it.

The feeling didn't last long. Dyer told us to turn out our pockets and give him the rest of our change. When Jerrod emptied his right front pocket, there among the pennies and nickels, were his car keys. *Damn!*

"Hey, clown. I'll take them, too," said Dyer. "I should've patted y'all down and found those a long time ago."

"I don't guess we were gonna have a chance to use those keys, anyway," said Jerrod.

"You're right, kid. See, you ain't so stupid."

"What happens now?" I asked.

"The boss is still working on it. Course, if it was up to me, I'd be having fun with you right now. But I can wait. He's gotta let me have you, sooner or later."

Dyer cackled, and I cringed. As he started out the door, he said, "See you, girls—soon, real soon."

He was just about to shut the door, when he flung it open again.

"I almost forgot. The boss said he wanted it dark in here. Looks like I better take that lamp."

Dyer took his gun out of his waistband and motioned us to the far side of the room. I looked over at the lamp sitting on the desk and my heart hit my tailbone. A few more steps and Dyer would notice what I could see clearly. Right below where the lamp was plugged into the wall socket, there was another cord. It was fat and black and disappeared behind the desk. Dyer was seconds away from discovering the drill and with it a partially completed hole in the wall and our passageway to freedom.

CHAPTER 26

They tell stories about me when I was little, before my dad died. Whenever we had company, my parents would parade me out to say hello before I got sent to bed. Every time, my dad would wink at our company and then ask me some question—like, if your model airplane landed on the roof, what would you do?

Invariably, I would trot out a whole long list of stuff: "Get a ladder," or "You should get a ladder, you're bigger," or "We could put Daisy on the roof, and she can hit it with her paw," or maybe, "I'll wait till it gets windy and blows the plane down. Anyway, I don't need an airplane. I can play with my train."

By this time, Dad and our company would be laughing and trying not to at the same time.

"I told you he was going to end up being a lawyer," he'd say. It wasn't till years later I understood what they'd found so funny. Then I started keeping my lists in my head.

Now, with Bill Dyer heading for the desk and certain disaster for us, there was no time for a list.

"Wait," I said, still trying to figure out what to say.

Dyer stopped and turned, a dark scowl on his face.

It came to me. I said, "If you unplug the lamp, it'll be dark. Aren't you afraid we'll overpower you in the dark?" Before Dyer could react to this, I raced for the light switch next to the door. I switched on the overhead fluorescent lights and then immediately rushed past Dyer to unplug the lamp. His mouth was still halfway open when I brought it to him.

"Here. Now all you have to do is switch off the lights before you close the door."

"You think you're smart, don't you? But you ain't so swift. Now you've reminded me about the big lights. Now I gotta do something about them, too. Or about you."

He opened the door and threw the lamp out into the mud. He pulled a cigarette lighter out of his pocket before switching off the lights. In the flickering glow of the lighter, his face looked even more sinister. He lifted the gun and pointed it directly at Jerrod, then at me. My legs got all rubbery and I closed my eyes, waiting to be dead. Nothing happened, so I opened my eyes again, and saw Dyer was still pointing the gun at us. He was grinning, obviously getting a lot of pleasure out of it.

"Bang," he said. Then he swung the gun to the side and placed the point of the barrel against the side of the light switch toggle.

In that small room, the crack of the gun was one of the loudest sounds I'd ever heard. My ears were ringing, and I could barely hear Dyer's laughter. It took a long time for him to bring himself under control. He said, "Good night, girls. Look at it this way, you'll have a lot more fun in the dark."

He hadn't quite managed to close the door when I heard excited voices outside. I caught the words, "Dammit, Bill. I said no bullets. I said wait till . . ."

Dyer interrupted with, "Not to worry, boss. The pussies are fine. I just . . ."

The thunk of the door shut off the rest. After the familiar sound of two locks being set, Jerrod and I were left in the darkness— again.

Jerrod said, "I thought we'd had it, Pete. I really did."

"Me, too."

"Pete?"

"Yes?"

"Did you hear what they were saying just before the door shut?"

"Afraid I did. Masterson wasn't so much upset about Dyer killing us, as he was about his using bullets. It's just a matter of time before they come back and arrange for us to have some kind of accident."

"Accident?"

"Think about it. With Pedro, the cops aren't going to look too hard. No family to report him missing. No clues to who he is. But with us, our parents are gonna notify the cops we're gone. Maybe they have already. Even if we completely disappear, there's going to be a heck of a manhunt."

"So what'll they do?"

"Don't you see? We've got to die in an accident. Something that'll keep them from looking any further. That's why they're taking so long. Oliver Masterson is trying to think up how to do it. I don't suppose it's something even he does every day."

"They've got to get rid of my car."

"That's it! What's better than a car accident?"

"Stubbing my toe would be better."

"I mean from their standpoint—it'd be perfect. Two careless teenagers in a new car. Driving too fast. It's perfect."

"Pete, let's get out of here."

We found our way to the desk and pulled it back. The first thing I did was unplug the drill and throw it completely under the desk. By feeling in the dark, we were able to locate the hole all right. But neither of us could find the hacksaw. As I was changing positions, I hit something and heard it skittering off into the darkness. *Damn.* "I think that was our saw."

We crawled around for a while, unable to find it. I was sweating like crazy. I kept listening for the sound of the key turning in the locks.

"Wish we had a lighter like Dyer's," said Jerrod. "Or matches."

"Wait a minute. There were two Bunsen burners. There's gotta be matches." I groped my way to where the Bunsen burners were. There was a drawer right under one of them. It didn't take long to hit something that rattled. A large box of matches. It took quite a bit of fumbling to get one lit. When I did, Jerrod dove for the hack saw and managed to pick it up before the match went out.

"Hey," I said. "Got another idea."

I lit another match and then turned the valve on one of the Bunsen burners. I heard a hiss of gas. Soon, we had a steady blue light. It was dim, but it was enough. I wondered how they had gas way out here in the country, but that mystery was solved when I looked under the workbench. There were two squat red propane bottles, one hooked up, the other a spare.

We went back to work on our hole. Little by little, triangle by triangle, we cut away the siding. The hole was almost big enough. *We're gonna do it!*

I celebrated a bit too soon. As I was handing the saw to Jerrod to finish the job, I heard faint voices through the opening.

"Shhh." I put my ear to the hole to listen. Sure enough the voices got louder, and I realized they were probably standing just around the corner by the door.

". . . got to drown . . . back to the creek. I hate to think it but, yeah, you can bash 'em one. But it's got to look like it happened in the accident . . . . No! Tony stays here with Juan and Carlina. He's not to be involved. It's bad enough I got Trav into this. Tony's out. Understand?"

The minute the key started to turn in the first lock, Jerrod and I jumped up and started to move the desk back. We had it in place before the second lock was opened. I started to dash for the Bunsen burner to turn it off, but I was too late. The door swung open, and I turned to face Oliver Masterson, with Bill Dyer right behind him.

"Very resourceful," said Masterson. "I see it's hard to keep you in the dark. Perhaps I *could* have used you in my operation, instead of Travis's lame-brained friend Mr. Brandon. But then, it wasn't his brains I needed."

I swallowed hard, then said, "It doesn't take much brains to realize it'd be stupid to drown us."

"Drown you? Where'd you get that idea?"

"I heard you. I . . ." Too late, I shut up as a puzzled frown crossed Masterson's face.

"You heard me, through a solid steel door?"

"No . . . I mean, in my mind, in my imagination I heard you. I figured since you tried to drown Pedro . . ."

"Ahh. Pedro. Now it all comes clear. Pedro refused to say where he'd been after he ran away. He was with you. It was stupid of him to run, with his brother and little sister still here, don't you think?"

"I think the only stupid thing he did was to come back."

Masterson tilted his head back and chuckled. "Perhaps you're right, young man. Perhaps you're right. Pedro wasn't supposed to die; Dyer got a little carried away, I'm afraid. So . . . if you're so smart, tell me—why would it be stupid to drown you?"

"Three drownings? Three people who knew each other? The police will suspect something. They'll nose around. Sooner or later, they'll find this place."

"Nonsense. Your friend here is a reckless driver. According to my sons, everyone at school knows he just got a new car. Would it be surprising if . . ."

He stared at me for a few seconds. His eyes softened, and for a minute he looked sad. He shook his head, slowly.

"Let's not talk about unpleasant things. Life's too short."

"Mine, you mean. And Jerrod's."

Masterson closed his eyes for a second, then shrugged.

"You are planning to kill us aren't you? To drown us."

His voice and his eyes got hard again. "I told you I didn't want to talk about it."

"It's okay to kill us but not to talk about it?"

"All right, you smart-ass little punk. Here's the deal. You're going to drive way too fast on a slippery road, go through the railing on the bridge approach, and end up in Diablo Creek. No one will be looking for anything. Trust me."

In one swift motion I grabbed one of the bottles of acetone and cocked it toward the flame of the burner. Bill Dyer pushed past his boss with his gun raised.

I thrust the bottle closer to the fire, glaring at Masterson. "When this place goes up in smoke, they'll come looking. Trust me."

"Put the bottle down," said Dyer. "You'll be dead long before you make a move."

"You might shoot me, but this place goes up anyway." I held the bottle close to the fire.

Oliver Masterson spoke up, "Back off, Bill. Let me handle this. All right, young man, put the bottle down."

"Why? What's the difference if he shoots me or if you drown me? Tell him to go outside. Then we'll talk."

"You really are a resourceful young man. Pity." He shook his head. "All right. Bill, outside."

The second Dyer had cleared the door I moved. I smashed the acetone bottle against the metal plate under the Bunsen burner. It broke and caught fire almost simultaneously, a small explosion. As Dyer ran back into the room, I threw the other acetone bottle at the floor in front of him and Masterson. It splashed all over both of them.

"Out!" shouted Masterson. "Clear of the fire or we'll go up like torches." He and Dyer scrambled and slipped in the slick, flammable liquid, flailing their arms and cussing. Masterson turned around in the doorway and shook his head. "You're going to wish you hadn't done that. You're going to wish like hell you'd just let it go."

With that, he pushed the door shut and locked it.

Within seconds, the smell of burning acetone was tearing at my lungs, and I started to cough. Jerrod was choking and sputtering, as we tried desperately to shove the desk aside. Finally it moved, and we threw ourselves behind it. Near the floor the air was clean, at least for the moment. There was more good news. The fire was creating a draft and pulling fresh moist air in through our escape hole. There was no problem with light now, either. The whole room was filled with a bright orange glow.

"Quick, saw out another piece. Just one more and we can make it."

Jerrod sawed like crazy while I watched the flames behind us. With a whoosh, the acetone I'd thrown on the floor caught fire. A blast of heat hit me, and I cowered against the wall next to my friend.

"Hurry. If the propane bottles go, we're cooked."

"Just . . . a . . . little . . . more. There! It's through."

I said, "You go first, I'm skinnier. If you make it, I know I can."

"But . . ."

"No time to argue. Just go."

Jerrod dove headfirst through the jagged hole. His head and shoulders got through fine, but his hips got stuck.

"Pete, I'm . . ."

"I'll push. You pull." I braced my back foot on the desk and shoved against Jerrod's legs. The desk started to slip, but I kept stretching out and pushing. Just before I lost all connection to the desk, Jerrod popped loose. He was free. I stuck my hands out and Jerrod grabbed onto me and pulled. I scraped my side on the rough wood as I went through, but I didn't care. I was outside in the fresh air, in a light rain. I'd never felt so good.

I lay in the mud, staring at the hole we'd just come through. The flames were clearly visible, and I shuddered to think about what would have happened if we'd been trapped. I pulled myself up and helped Jerrod to his feet. It was then we heard the ominous click of metal. I froze. A second later a beam of light hit me in the face. Oliver Masterson's voice came oozing out of the darkness behind it.

"Well, well, well. I don't know how you fellows did it, but you keep managing to surprise me. I guess Plan B isn't going to work out after all. We'll have to go back to Plan A. Looks like you boys are going to get your drowning after all."

CHAPTER 27

liver Masterson ordered Jerrod and me to march to the office, "and make it quick!"

"You heard the man. Move your butts." Bill Dyer wanted us to know he was there in the darkness, too, with his gun trained on us.

The office was a scene of total chaos. Travis and Bulldog were pulling out desk drawers full of papers and stacking them near the door. A closet had been emptied of clothes. Boxes of personal stuff were scattered all over the floor. I guessed they were expecting the fire to draw the attention of the authorities. They were removing anything that might tie any of them to the drug lab.

"Let's get this safe out to Travis's pickup," said Masterson. "It's going to take all four of us to load it. Bill—stick these kids in the bedroom with the others."

"What for?"

"Because you've got to lay the gun down, to help lift this thing." He shook his head. "And when you drop these two off, bring back a blanket. We can use it to drag the safe out."

Dyer opened the door to the long corridor and motioned us in with a wave of his gun. At the far end were three doors. One, on the right, was partially open, and I could see it was a small bathroom with a sink and a rust-stained toilet. The door on the left

129

was closed, fastened shut with a large sliding dead-bolt. Straight ahead was another bolted door. In his low, crackly voice, Dyer told me to open it.

We walked into a room similar in size to the office. The only items of furniture were three twin beds and a rickety table with chairs. A stack of clothes and a few dishes, cups, and silverware were on the floor in a corner. A second door, next to the one we came in, opened onto another small toilet. I guess the third door out in the hallway also connected with this bathroom, but it was locked from the outside.

Juan and Carlina sat together on a bed, their already small figures hunched down even further. They were holding each other, shivering and looking scared. I don't suppose they had any idea what was happening.

Tony Masterson sat at the table. "What's going on?" he asked.

"We're clearing out," said Dyer. "The lab's on fire."

Tony started for the door.

"No." Dyer held up his hand. "Your dad wants you here till we're ready to move."

"This is crazy. My own father is keeping me prisoner?"

"Just for a minute. We're loading stuff in the cars." He left and we could hear the dead-bolt slide into place.

Tony threw a bewildered look at Jerrod and me. "I still don't know what's going on."

I said, "You know what this place is? What they do here?"

Tony nodded his head, slowly. "Just found out. Still can't believe it."

"You didn't know about any of this?"

"I'm not blind. I figured out a long time ago Travis was . . . was up to no good. I'd even guessed it had something to do with drugs. But this?" He swung his hands around, palms up. "*Making* the stuff? And my own father in charge?"

"How could you not know?"

"Dad buys and sells stuff. Electronic equipment. He's always going off, but I thought it was on buying trips."

Tony looked like he might cry any second. "Dad always said if he caught me doing drugs, he'd kill me." He gestured around the room, looking bewildered. "I can't believe all this."

"It gets worse," I said. "You know about Pedro?"

"Who's Pedro?"

I looked over at Jerrod and then launched into the whole story. I talked as fast as I could, not knowing when Dyer would return with his sadistic grin and his loaded gun.

Tony sat frozen in his chair, white-faced. I saw a tear making its way down his cheek.

I went over and tried to talk to Juan. "Are you all right?" When I got a confused look, I tried again in my lousy Spanish. He shook his head, then nodded, then shook his head no again. I couldn't blame him for being confused.

"Tell me what happened to Pedro?" I said.

Carlina started to cry louder. Juan's face tensed into an angry scowl. I saw fear and what looked like shame in Carlina's face.

"Did Dyer . . ."

Juan nodded. "And the other two. Pedro tried to stop them. Pedro tried to keep them away from our sister."

Carlina's cries got louder. She said, between sobs, "I told him it was no use. They were too strong."

"What happened? Tell me."

Juan spoke up. "Pedro and I were tied with ropes while *Señor* Dyer and then the others did . . . while they did what they wanted to do with Carlina. Pedro got loose. He started to beat *Señor* Dyer with his hands."

Juan stopped and rubbed his eyes. Then he said, "Carlina, she tried to run away then, but Dyer put the gun to Pedro's head. He told her to come back or he would shoot her brother."

Carlina turned away, hiding her face in her hands.

Juan went on. "When Carlina started back, Pedro shouted to her, 'no, no,' but she came anyway. Pedro pushed Dyer away and started to run to Carlina, but Dyer shouted and grabbed Pedro's arm. He threw him into the wall. Carlina and I, we ran to hold our Pedrito, but it was no good. No good. He was dead. *Muerto*."

I put my hand on Juan's shoulder and looked at Carlina. I didn't know the Spanish for "I'm sorry," so I said it in English. Juan and Carlina seemed to understand.

Juan said, "When *Señor* Masterson he came, he was very angry. Then they took Pedro away."

I went back to where Tony Masterson was sitting and told him, "That's how Pedro's body got in the creek."

Tony closed his eyes, fighting to hold back tears.

I was having trouble controlling my own emotions. I lashed out at Tony, wanting to hurt him for being so clueless. "You didn't know you had a rapist for a brother, did you? Or did you? Maybe that's how you and Travis got your kicks . . ."

"No! I don't know why you're saying this. I didn't know. I didn't know any of this."

I was calmer now, and felt a surge of sympathy for Tony. Still, he had to learn what kind of a family he was in.

I grabbed him by the shoulders and shook him. "There's more, Tony. It gets worse. Bill Dyer and your father told Jerrod and me they intend to arrange an 'accident' for us. We're going to end up in Jerrod's car down in Diablo Creek—drowned." I looked over at the two Nicaraguans, huddled on the bed. "I'm guessing those two aren't any more use to your father, either, what with the lab burning up."

"But they can't . . ."

"What've they got to lose now? These two'll probably end up like their brother."

Tony was crying openly now. This was too much, coming at him all at once. He clutched his arms to his sides and curled up like someone being stoned by an angry mob. I understood how he felt.

"You've gotta help us, Tony," said Jerrod. You're the only one who can."

Tony shook his head, and said in a small voice, "How can I? My father, my brother, they'll go to jail, or worse. My family . . . how could I do that to my family?"

I barked, "Your family is *killing* people. And not just with the drugs. Up to now, you haven't been involved. If you go along with this, you'll be part of it. You understand? Can you live with it on your conscience, Tony?"

"I just can't. I can't."

"You'll be charged with murder, just like them. Don't you see, the lab's burning down. I'm sure they'll be able to tell from the ashes what was going on . . ."

There was a huge blast of sound. The walls shook. The furniture bounced.

"The propane tanks! Must've blown," I shouted after I'd recovered my voice.

Within minutes, a corner of the bedroom began to heat up, and the paint on the wall started to turn brown. A piece of the burning lab had apparently blown against our own building. Tony and Jerrod started banging on the door and shouting for someone to come and let us out. Carlina and Juan and I pressed close together as far as possible from the charring wall, which suddenly burst into open flame. It wouldn't be long before the smoke would get us. *Again! How can this be happening again?* I yelled for everyone to get as close to the floor as possible. Juan and Carlina didn't respond, so I pulled them down.

The door opened and Jerrod and Tony stumbled through. Dyer, gun in hand, took in the scene. He shouted at me to get out. I crawled through the doorway, but when Juan and Carlina tried to follow, Dyer shoved them back roughly with his foot. He pushed the door closed and threw the dead-bolt, leaving two young Nicaraguans to die, consumed by the flames.

As we were being herded through the office and out the front door, I looked at Tony and jerked my head back toward the burning bedroom, pleading with him to do something about Juan and Carlina. He turned away from me.

Outside, we could still hear the sounds of screaming and pounding echoing down the hallway and through the office. Tony cried out and bolted back into the building and down the corridor toward the frantic Nicaraguans.

"Stop him!" yelled Oliver Masterson.

They all looked at each other, waiting for someone else to move.

"You, Travis," said Masterson, in a suddenly quiet, resigned voice. "Please go and get your brother."

Travis hesitated, watching his father who stood in the rain rubbing his eyes. Masterson sighed when he realized Travis was standing still.

His voice hardened. "Go, boy!"

Before Travis had a chance to move, however, Tony was back, staring at the ground.

"Check the door, Travis," said Masterson, quietly again. "If he unlocked it, well . . . lock it again."

"Dad, I don't want . . ."

"Do it, Trav. I don't want this, either, but we don't have a choice. Don't you see? We have no choice now. None."

Travis walked to the hallway door, with his head down. It was quiet now. The desperate shouting and the pounding had stopped. Travis called back. "I can see the dead-bolt from here, Dad. He didn't unlock it."

"I was going to," said Tony, "but I knew it wasn't any use. You'd just shove them back in and lock it again."

Tony gave me a look that seemed to say, "I'm sorry. Forgive me."

I wasn't about to, though. He was right about them locking it again, of course, but he should have at least *tried*.

"Get in there." Masterson ordered Jerrod and me into Bill Dyer's car. "Tony, you ride with me. Travis, you and Bulldog take your truck and go find Jerrod's car. When you do, wait at the end of the drive."

It took only a few minutes for the lights of two cars to stop out on the road, and we heard a faint honk.

"Let's move," Masterson shouted from his car window. "I've got a place we can go while we take care of these two."

Dyer drove with his gun in one hand. As we started down the driveway, I turned back. The lab was almost gone. The fire and then the explosion had left very little, but what was left was burning furiously. I wasn't looking at the lab, though. I was looking at the center building, whose front corner was now burning, too. I was looking at the center building where I could picture a young man and his sister huddled on the floor, trying to escape the heat and the smoke for as long as they possibly could.

CHAPTER 28

We drove back down the farm road toward town. Dyer was in front, with Jerrod and me sitting next to him. Dyer's gun never left his hand. Oliver Masterson and Tony were in the next car, Travis's pickup behind him, and Bulldog in the rear, driving Jerrod's Firebird.

I had no idea what time it was, but guessed it was at least a couple of hours after midnight. I didn't think it likely anyone would see us. If they did, they probably wouldn't give it much thought. It was raining harder now. Lightning flickered in the distance.

As we neared the Diablo Creek bridge, the mobile phone in Dyer's car buzzed. He answered, "Yeah?"

After listening for a minute, he said, "Got it. Okay, boss, I remember. I think I see it ahead."

Just before the bridge we swung left off the road. As our headlights swept through the darkness, I caught sight of the dilapidated old barn where Jerrod and I had hidden earlier. *Has it only been a few hours since we'd poked through the rubble, scaring rats and mice?* It seemed like forever.

We all parked in back. Dyer jumped out and ran around to the passenger side. He threw open the door and jerked us out onto the ground. Oliver Masterson pulled us to our feet and herded us into the old barn, Tony trailing behind. Masterson and Dyer carried flashlights. They shone them around the walls and the sagging ceiling. As terrified as I was, my mind registered things we hadn't seen when we'd hidden there earlier at sunset, without lights. There were rusted old hand tools and shreds of what once were gunny sacks hanging from the walls. The roof sagged because of the broken beam, but it was still intact. There were only two tiny windows, way up high, but the walls were perforated with holes. Below each opening, dark streaks of rotting wood glistened with new moisture.

I heard two car doors slam. The next flash of lightning showed Travis and Bulldog silhouetted in the barn's doorway taking in the scene. Masterson ignored them, pointed the light at a clear spot on the floor and ordered Jerrod and me to sit there.

"Here's what we do. Travis and Tony'll take everything we salvaged to our storage place. Dyer and I'll walk back to the bridge and plan something for these two. Not gonna be easy."

"Hell," said Dyer. "Just knock 'em in the head, strap 'em in the car, and roll it into the creek. No problem."

"The car has to be going fast enough to break through the guardrail. That means one of us has to drive it into the rail and jump out at the last minute. Volunteers?"

I huddled with my friend on the floor. On the ride over here, I'd been scared, sure, but it had all been hazy—like I was watching a movie, not being driven to the place where I was expected to die. But now these guys were planning our cold-blooded murder while we sat a few feet away listening. As far as Masterson was concerned, Jerrod and I were already dead.

After a minute of silence, Bulldog spoke up. "Couldn't we wire the gas pedal down and let her go?"

"Oh, that's very bright, Mr. Brandon. This is supposed to be an *accident*, remember? Besides, I want these two strapped in with seat belts. By all accounts, no one'll believe they were stupid enough to be out on a country road in the rain without seat belts."

You got that right. But then, why would we be out in the country at three in the morning in the first place?

Oliver Masterson must have read my mind. "Unless, of course, they've been drinking. Oh, yes. If they were drinking, drinking hard—they might've gone joy-riding in Wilson's shiny new car— and without seat belts."

He nodded rapidly now, apparently pleased with this new thought. "If one of them isn't strapped into the driver's seat, one of us can drive the car into the guardrail more easily. Travis, here's what you'll do. After you and Tony drop things off at the storage place, go home and get a bottle of bourbon. Don't go into the house. I don't want to wake your mother. Get it out of the pool house. A full one—we need these two to be really wasted."

By now, Tony was walking like a zombie. Travis had to take his brother by the arm to lead him outside. I heard a door to the pickup open and slam shut. After a minute, we heard Travis's voice again. "Dad, can I talk to you for a minute? Alone?"

"All right, but make it quick. We gotta get this done before dawn. Bill, Bulldog, take a hike."

Grumbling, Dyer and Brandon went out into the rain. Again I realized Masterson had stopped thinking of Jerrod and me as *people.* He considered himself alone with his son, even though we were sitting right there on the floor.

Travis said, "I don't think it's a good idea for Tony to go home with me to get the booze. I don't trust him. You've kept him out of the whole business because you didn't think he had the stomach for it. Right?"

"Right. But more than that. Listen, Travis, I never even wanted *you* in. Somehow you got in. I didn't like it, but . . . but it seemed to suit you. Tony, though, he's different; he's like your ma."

"So, what're you saying, Dad? Tony's good, and I'm bad? Is that it?"

"I'm just saying . . ."

"I know what you're saying."

Travis stalked around in a circle, then went nose to nose with his father. "You're saying when you look at me, you see yourself. Don't you?"

"I guess you're . . ."

"And you know what, Dad? You're right. This little boy'll do *anything* his old man wants."

"You've always been special to me."

"That's bull. Tony's the one you've always treated like he was special. Given him anything he ever wanted."

"I've given you *both* everything. A big house, a swimming pool, your truck. I didn't want you to have it like I did."

Travis's voice oozed sarcasm. "Tell me again, Dad, about picking melons when you were twelve and about your only pair of pants and all that other junk."

"It was like that! What do you think all this has been for? I've struggled my whole life to pull myself up so you could . . ."

"So Tony could!"

"No, it's you I've had by my side—in everything."

"Well, congratulations, Dad. You killed a couple of kids tonight, and you made *me* make sure they died." Travis was crying now. "And I did, I did . . . you were right. Every friggin' thing you've ever asked me to do, I did."

Masterson and Travis faced each other, breathing heavily. Jerrod and I were still invisible on the floor.

Regaining his tone of authority, Masterson said, "We still have to do something about Tony. I made a mistake, bringing him with me tonight. I should've taken him home when Dyer called me on my cell phone, but . . . I thought he'd stay in the car and keep his nose clean. Now he's in. I sure as hell don't like it."

"He's still a Boy Scout, Dad. If I take him home, he'll split and try to stop us. I know him even better than you."

"Do you have another idea?"

"Yes. Keep him here. Keep him with you till we finish it with Wilson and Grayson. There won't be any reason for Tony to squeal then, and . . . besides, he'll be part of it. Guilty like the rest of us. Like his big brother. Your precious little Tony'll be no better'n me then, Dad. He'll have to keep quiet."

Masterson stamped around, cursing. He said to Travis, "How did it come to this? How in hell did it get so out of hand? It was one thing having you and your buddy Bulldog help in the business. But y'all couldn't keep your pants zipped, and Dyer lost it with Pedro. Now the other two, and this."

Travis's voice cut through the darkness. "It's a bit late to get soft. And don't worry, *Father*. Your chip-off-the-old-block son can handle this. I can handle Little Brother, too. All we have to do is keep his nose right in the middle of it, till it's all over."

Masterson paced around for a while, kicking at the rubbish on the floor. Finally, he said, "Okay, Travis, I guess you're right. Take Bulldog—and hurry. I want this finished."

Car doors slammed, and the sound of Travis's pickup retreated toward the road. Tony shuffled into the barn.

"Dad, I want to . . ."

"Shut up, Tony. I need to think."

It got quiet. The only sound was a low rustling from under the piles of trash. *Rodents? Snakes?*

"I'm going down to the bridge by myself," Masterson finally said. "Watch them, Dyer, these two have a habit of pulling surprises."

"I ain't standing here in the dark like a freaking nursemaid."

"Then sit."

"No way! There's things in here."

"So, that's your problem. Big Bad Bill is scared of mice."

"Rats."

"Very well," said Masterson. "Big Bad Bill is afraid of rats."

"Damn right I am."

"Then I suggest you stand outside the door in the rain."

When Masterson had gone, Dyer said, "Hell. I'm gonna sit in the car. But don't get any ideas, pussies. The window will be rolled down, and this baby," he waved his gun, "will be pointed square at the door. C'mon, Tony."

"I'm staying here."

"Suit yourself." Dyer went out to his car, and we heard the door slam. A minute later the strains of country/western music blasted out for a second before being cranked down quiet.

I whirled toward Tony and said, "Thanks for all your help, guy. How does it feel to be responsible for two people roasting to death because you were too chicken to stop it?"

"But I did."

"What?"

"I did help them, at least I hope I did."

"C'mon. Don't give us a line of bull. I heard Travis say you hadn't opened the dead-bolt. The door was still locked."

"The one he could see. I knew someone'd check the lock on the main door, so I opened the one on the side—the one to the bathroom. I figured nobody'd notice that one was open. I was right."

"Oh, man, Tony, I'm sorry. Sorry for what I been thinking about you."

"Just hope they found it. I knocked on the bathroom door so maybe those kids'd think to crawl in there. But . . . who knows if they heard me. You know how bad the smoke was already when we got out."

After a minute, I said, "Tony, thanks for trying to save Juan and Carlina. Think you could do the same for Jerrod and me?"

"Sure. I'd try, but I don't know what to do. My father'll be back soon. That man Dyer is right outside with a gun. And I don't see any other way out of here."

"If there was, would you let us go?"

"Course I would. You can't believe how I feel with all this . . . all this going down. I wanted to do what Dad said, stick with him, you know . . . protect my brother. But this . . . I'll help. If I can."

"There is another door," I said.

"I didn't see one," said Tony.

"Me, neither," said Jerrod. "All those holes in the walls—they're way too small to get through. We'd make all kinds of noise trying to bust out. Dyer'd be on us in a second."

"It's not in the walls. It's in the floor."

"Oh, no, oooh, no," said Jerrod. "No way I'm gettin' into that thing."

Tony said, "I don't get it. What're you talking about? I didn't see anything."

"We were here earlier. There's a kind of trap door in the floor. It's under some of the trash."

"Count me out," said Jerrod.

"Uh, uh. You're in. C'mon, Jerrod, help me find it."

I crawled in the dark to the center of the room, with Jerrod, grumbling, behind me. On my knees, leaning forward, I swept my hands around in big circles.

"Damn." A splinter of wood jammed up under my fingernail. It hurt like crazy, but I forced the pain out of my mind. I kept searching till I found the pile of junk I thought had been leaning against the door when we'd pried it open earlier. With my fingers raw and probably bleeding I searched the floor for a crack. *There. Found it.*

"C'mon, Jerrod, help me pull it up."

In the darkness, I could hear Jerrod breathing raggedly. He wasn't moving.

"Over here, now!" I said, sharply. Even in my own ears, I sounded like somebody else. But what could I do? We *had* to move, and we had to move fast.

It seemed like forever, but finally, I could hear Jerrod's labored breathing next to me. I reached for him and pulled him down to the floor.

We didn't have anything sharp to wedge into the crack like before, and I didn't want to take time to find something in the dark. We had to pry with our fingers. I wasn't sure we could do it, and the pain was about as bad as I could take. Finally, though, we managed to move it up enough to get a finger under it, then a hand.

"Tony," I said. "This is where you come in. Crawl over. Help us hold this up."

When we were all standing with the door upright, I said to Jerrod, "You ready?"

"I can't, Pete. I just can't."

"I don't get it. You've never been scared of anything. I was the one. You had to drag me to see the flood. Right?"

"This is different. I can't stand not bein' able to see."

"Ya gotta do it, Jerrod."

"Nooh. Can't . . . do it. No . . . I can't, I just . . ."

"I'll go first. Find out what's down there. All right?"

He stopped protesting and sniffled for a while. Then, in a voice I could barely hear, he said, "Okay."

I was taking a chance going first. If he still refused, he'd be in deep trouble, and probably so would I. Not much choice, though—if we were going to go, I was going to have to lead the way.

I told Jerrod, when I was down I'd stand to the left, and he should jump in on the right so he wouldn't kill me.

"Tony, once we're down, lower the door back. Don't let it drop. It makes a hell of a noise if you drop it. Then try to shove some of this junk on top of it, so they don't notice it right away."

"They're gonna be all over this building and all around it. If you can't get away . . . it'll be just a few minutes before . . ."

"I know. But it's our only chance. After you've hidden the door, just—I dunno—lay on the floor. Pretend we hit you over the head or something."

Moving around in the dark, Jerrod and I sat with our legs dangling into the hole. I was on the left, with Jerrod sitting to my right. There was an ugly smell coming up from below, the stench of dead things rotting. I tried to look down into the pit, but there was nothing but blackness. Big surprise. We couldn't even see each other here in the barn.

I said, "You be careful, Tony. Dyer's gonna be one pissed dude. And . . . Tony?"

"Yeah?"

"Thanks."

I swung myself backwards over the edge, supporting myself on my elbows. My feet dangled in the air, touching nothing.

"Hang on to me, Jerrod. I've got to get lower."

"I don't like this; who knows what's down there."

"No choice," I said. "I know what's up here."

Slowly, Jerrod helped me lower myself until I was hanging by my fingers. Still nothing but air. It was crunch time. Everything that'd happened before—threatened by fire, a gun at my head— none of it could match the fear I was feeling now. I thought about giving it all up. I thought it'd be easier just to let them do what they were planning to do. I wanted more than I've ever wanted anything in my life to crawl out of that hole.

Instead, I loosened my fingers, letting them slip off of the splintery edge. And then I was dropping—falling into a deeper darkness than any I'd ever known.

CHAPTER 29

Time is a strange thing. Hours can seem like minutes, and seconds can stretch into forever when you're falling. I bent my legs to absorb the shock of whatever lay below me. When I hit bottom, the landing was surprisingly soft. *Water!* Before I could react, I was totally under and spluttering with the foul taste of putrid liquid. I tried to stand but couldn't tell up from down. I thrashed around wildly until my knees got planted in something not quite solid, an oozy muck that pulled on me like quicksand. It was only a few inches thick, though, and it was enough to tell me which way to find oxygen. I struggled upright, finally able to breathe. The air was so heavy with the stench of decay, I wished I didn't have to.

"Pete? You all right?"

"I think so."

"I heard splashing."

"Yeah. Water's about chest deep. That's good, I think. Your turn."

"What if there's dead snakes and rats and stuff floating around?"

Even though I'd been worrying about the same thing, I said, "Hey, it's fine. Water's clean. C'mon." If he backed out now, we'd both be caught again. I'd have jumped into the darkness for

145

nothing—and there was no way I was going to go through that for *nothing*.

While Jerrod grunted and cursed as he hung himself over the edge, I pressed up against the wall away from where I thought he'd be dropping. Since I couldn't see him, I had to go by sound, but it was bouncing around in there, so I wasn't sure where Jerrod was. Maybe he'd come down right on top of me and break my neck.

When he fell, he missed my neck but grazed my side and shoved me hard into the wall of the pit. I hit my head and felt dizzy for a second, but it passed. I was able to help Jerrod struggle to his feet, coughing and spluttering.

He said, "Oh, yuck. This stuff's awful. I don't like this." At least he was functioning now, complaining, not paralyzed by his fear.

I called out, "We're down, Tony, close her up."

We heard a whisper from above, "Okay," and then the sound of the door being lowered into place. After some scraping noises, it was quiet. All we could hear was our breathing and a slow plink, plink in the dark.

"Feel around the walls. It's gotta go somewhere. I can hear water dripping."

"Over here, Pete. There's a hole, a big round hole."

Following Jerrod's voice, I moved beside him and felt around with my hands until I'd decided it was the end of a large culvert, made of crinkly corrugated metal. The water level was high enough so there was only a foot or so of air space right in the middle. By stooping down and tilting my head back, I could just manage to move in a short way, but it was a killer.

"We might as well try it." I crept along. Leaning forward at that awkward angle, my back felt like it was going to break. I hated to put my hands into that mucky bottom, but there was no other way I could make any progress. It was slow, but little by little we moved along in the foul water, me in front, Jerrod cussing and sloshing behind. *I think we're gonna make it.*

I was confident, savoring freedom ahead, when I realized my breathing space was getting smaller! The culvert was dipping down deeper into the water. Soon there'd be no air space at all.

"Damn."

"Whatsa matter, Pete?"

"We're trapped. It goes under water."

"I knew it! I knew we shouldn't have come down here. I knew it."

I said, "Guess it goes to the creek. When this building was new, they must've used this pipe to get rid of waste stuff. Or maybe it was the other way around. Maybe it was like a well."

"Why did we come down here? Oh, man."

"I wonder how far it goes."

"Maybe we can holler at Tony. He'll help us climb out."

"If I knew it didn't go very far, I'd swim underwater."

Jerrod started to shout, "Tony! Tony!"

"No! Shut up, Jerrod. Just shut up and let me think."

"What's to think? We're trapped. You said so your . . ."

"Jerrod. Use your brain! We climb back up, we're dead. I've gotta try this."

"Yeah, but you don't make it, you drown."

"I know. I know. Even if it's not too far, the end might be buried in the mud, covered with a grate—who knows."

"So whatta we do, Pete? Just wait here, hope they'll give up and go away?"

"I don't think there's a chance in hell they'll do that. They'll find the trap door eventually."

"We're hiding in the pipe. It's dark."

"Jeez, Jerrod. They've got flashlights. When Masterson makes Dyer climb down here, we'll be like a couple of guppies in a fish bowl."

I decided to risk a little underwater exploration. I imagined myself somewhere down the pipe, half out of air, desperately trying to turn so I could get back. Not a pretty picture. I decided to turn around to begin with and push myself backwards. That way, when I felt I was in danger of running out of air, I could swim forward quickly to where Jerrod waited.

The first try was just a short one, a few feet, to get the feel of it. The next one was longer. I still didn't come out in the open, but I had breath left when I shot back to where I started and ran into Jerrod.

One more try. This time I was going to push myself as far and as hard as I could. I took three deep breaths and then ducked under. Using the corrugated sides of the pipe, I shoved myself along. Just as I'd reached the point where I absolutely had to turn back, I felt the sideways push of water against my legs. Kicking upward against the top of the culvert I hit—nothing. I'd made it!

At least I thought I'd made it. It was decision time again, and this time I *had* to think fast. If I tried for the surface and found I was in the creek, everything would be great. If I was wrong and couldn't reach the surface, I was going to die right there. With the air I had left, there'd be no way to dive down and get back to where my friend waited. But then, getting caught by Dyer and Masterson again was certain death. I turned and swam upward.

I almost couldn't believe it when I popped through to the surface. My chest hurt, and I was gasping for breath. There wasn't enough air in the whole state of Texas to satisfy my lungs. It was raining hard, beating down on my head. A flash of lightning illuminated the dark silhouette of the building up the hill to my right. Straight ahead, the outline of the bridge came into view for a brief second.

Jerrod. I had to get back to Jerrod and bring him out. But I'd lost the entrance to the culvert! Over and over I forced myself underwater, desperately searching with my feet. Nothing. Dog-paddling in place, I forced myself to calm down so I could think. I'd probably drifted with the current. Swimming upstream, I tried again, then again. Still nothing! I thrashed my way into shallower water where I could stand. I kept on striking out with my legs, churning the water in frustration. Finally, I hit something—a low hump in the muddy floor of the creek bed. Following it out toward deeper water, I began to feel the corrugated ribs and finally reached the end. Clinging to the pipe, it took forever to calm down. But I had to. My friend was still in there.

Two more underwater swims! All I wanted to do was head downstream as fast and as far as I could, but I needed to make the journey through the pipe twice more. I took more deep breaths, grateful for my training as a runner. Then I was back in the pipe, swimming like crazy. I nearly creamed Jerrod when I ran into him.

He was crying. "Pete! Oh, God, Pete . . . I thought you were dead."

"I'm here, Jerrod."

"You didn't come back . . . I thought . . . dead. Oh, Pete."

"Not yet, Jerrod. Not dead yet. And guess what? I found the end. I was outside, breathing fresh air. I found it! C'mon, give me a second to get my breath again, then let's go."

"I don't think I can do it. Underwater? In the dark, with dead stuff?"

"No worse'n where we are."

"I never liked swimming underwater."

"But you can if you have to. And, Jerrod . . . *you have to.* Besides, this isn't really swimming. It's just pulling yourself along the pipe. You can do it, man. I did it backwards."

"I still don't think . . ."

"Jerrod! You got two choices. You go with me, *now,* or you stay here. By yourself. In the dark." He went.

I pushed along right behind him. A couple of times I had to shove him, urging him to move faster. Again I felt the welcome force of fresh water pushing sideways. As I surfaced, I collided with Jerrod, treading water and inhaling and exhaling in great noisy breaths. I started to say something, when I heard shouting up by the old barn.

"I hear something in the water. Down there."

"Where?"

"In the creek. Right below us."

Two flashlights shone through the rain, sweeping back and forth. Just then, another burst of lightning showed two people standing at the top of the bank, their feet spread wide.

"I see 'em," called the gravelly voice. "It's the kids." Dyer. With the gun.

"Jerrod. Quick! We gotta get under. Follow me."

I dove and swam with the current as far as I could. I heard Jerrod surface again just before I did. For a guy who claimed he'd never learned to swim underwater, the threat of getting shot was a good teacher.

Up on the bank, the flashlights were moving like cobra's heads, searching for prey.

"Under again! Keep going."

As we moved downstream, coming to the surface only long enough for another quick breath, we saw the lights and heard Dyer and Masterson running along the side of the creek, trying to get ahead of us. Once, one of the lights stopped, and just as I dove under, I heard the muted pop of a gun and, at the same time, felt a shock wave hit my face. *Jerrod. Did Jerrod get hit?*

Crazy things came to mind. Maybe I'd been hit myself. I'd seen movies where people went a long time and then could hardly believe it when they saw blood pouring out of themselves.

When I'd surfaced and dived again and surfaced, for what seemed like hours, I heard from up on the bank, "Damn. Watch it! Barbed wire."

I shouted at Jerrod, when I heard him splashing nearby. "You all right?"

"I . . . think . . . so."

"Sounds like they're stopped. Fence. But it won't be for long. Let's move it."

We swam, then, like the devil was chasing us. I guess you could say he was. I don't know where the energy came from, but we managed to keep going. Gradually, the shouting and cursing of Masterson and Dyer died into the distance as the waters of Diablo Creek carried us away. Soon, we could see small houses, their blue and pink and white exteriors lit by the pale glare of streetlights.

With almost no strength left, we hauled ourselves up onto a gravel road, a welcome and familiar gravel road. The flickering lightning made it stand out in bold relief above the black expanse of fields still wet from the flood. It looked like a giant gray ribbon, an arrow pointing straight for Bennington's Northside, and home.

CHAPTER 80

. . . so, anyway, Dad, that's the story. I'm glad I told you about it. Of course, if you're really in some place where they deliver mail from surviving sons, I suppose you'd probably know all about what's going on here anyway. Cosmic television or something.

Let's face it, I haven't been writing all this stuff for you. I've been doing it for me. And it's been good. It really has. It's stupid, I guess, 'cause you haven't gotten back to me, haven't given me any signs, or anything, but I feel a lot less guilty. Forgiven maybe. Not by you, exactly, but by myself—for not being the kid you needed when you were getting sick. And, by the way, I forgive you for doing what you must have had to do, there near the end.

Funny thing, though, the more I write, the less I feel the need to write. Somehow, and I don't suppose you'll be upset about this— somehow, sending my thoughts to an eight-year-old memory is starting to feel—irrelevant. Especially now, when there's a real, flesh-and-blood person waiting for me down at the DQ.

So long, Dad. I won't be writing again, but I'll think about you often.

Your son, Pete

CHAPTER 31

The Dairy Queen was nearly empty. That suited me just fine. Jennifer James and I sat in a booth near the back. She patted the cracked red leather seat, and I slid in next to her. She twisted toward me, leaning on the table, so she could look me in the eyes as I talked. I didn't need much encouragement.

"I heard Mr. Masterson's been arrested," she said.

"Uh huh. And Travis. And Bulldog. Dyer took off, and they think he left the state. They'll catch him, though."

"What happened to the two Nicaraguans?"

"They found 'em hiding in the bushes. By the time the firemen got there, the whole place had gone up, and the fire was dying down all by itself."

"Poor kids." Jennifer's eyes were bright with moisture. "I still don't understand how the three of them got here in the first place."

"Far as they can tell, they were special-ordered by Oliver Masterson."

"What do you mean?"

"I mean, you know the guys who try to make a living smuggling human beings into this country?"

"Sure."

"Usually they're paid by the people who're being smuggled. It's a pretty cruel business, 'cause people cough up their last peso and then get dumped along the border somewhere. Most of the time they get caught and sent back. Then they have nothing."

"So what about Carlina and her brothers?"

"Like I said, special-ordered. Masterson paid these 'coyotes' to find him three people—young, no families, no one who'd miss them. When the guy found the three of them in Managua, begging in the streets, it was perfect. The only family they had were each other, and they'd all be together under Masterson's thumb. Like slaves."

"Where are Carlina and Juan now?"

"In Houston, being held by the INS, the government immigration people."

"To send back to Nicaragua?"

"Maybe not. Jerrod's folks have written letters, gotten some big shots involved. They're trying to get them asylum, let them stay here. Even my mom's tried to help."

"You sound surprised."

"Not really, she's a good person. It's just that by going to bat for them, she's sorta saying it was right for *me* to try to help them. Are you hungry? Want something to go with that shake?"

"No, I'm fine."

"Anyway, right after I got home . . . when all the fuss had died down, and I'd made my statement to the police, Mom broke down and cried and screamed at me, 'Don't you ever do anything like that again!' She kept on yelling, over and over, 'Do you hear? Do you hear me?' "

"That's not hard to understand."

"Yeah. Then I surprised myself. Instead of pulling into my shell, or trying to run away, I walked over and put my arm around her— held her till she calmed down. Then she said something I can still hardly believe. She said, 'You did a good thing, Peter, a good thing.' Then she sniffled, gave me a sad little smile, and left my room."

Jennifer took my hand, then dropped it on the table. With her forefinger, she slowly traced the outline of my fingers, then looked up and grinned.

"School's gonna be pretty dull for you, isn't it?"

"I don't know about that. Tomorrow I'm thinking of demanding an apology from Principal Hyatt. That should be fun. Then, last period, I intend to go out and kick some butt at volleyball."

Jennifer laughed and ran her finger down my chest.

"You know what, Peter? I believe you will. I believe it's guar-an-teed."

ABOUT THE AUTHOR

In his prior life, Ted Simmons enjoyed a career as an oil company technology manager. Most of this time was spent in international producing operations, providing him with the opportunity to live and work in some of the world's most fascinating places. He developed a keen interest in the cultures and beliefs of other people and thinks many Americans would benefit from some of his insights.

Ted and his family lived in the jungles of Sumatra, Indonesia, the suburbs of London, and the desert region known as the "Neutral Zone" between Saudi Arabia and Kuwait. He has trod the ancient Silk Road in Central Asia (Uzbekistan, Turkmenistan, Kazakhstan, Azerbaijan), stood in the columned halls of the Temple of Karnak in Egypt, jostled with crowds atop the Great Wall of China, crawled through tunnels dug by the North Vietnamese during the war, and hunted butterflies with his teenage son in the mountains of Taiwan.

The novel, *Diablo Creek,* was derived from events in the news during Ted's time living in one of the suburbs of Houston, Texas. The story is fictional; the conditions that inspired it are, unfortunately, very real.

Ted Simmons is active in the writing community. He was Chairman of the Houston Writers' Conference in 2000, is currently Past-President of the Tallahassee Writers' Association, and chaired the association's nationwide Seven Hills Contest for Writers.

Ted's first novel, *Sandstorm,* also from CyPress Publications, was a 2006 *ForeWord Magazine* Book of the Year Award nominee.

WHITE HEAT, WHITE ASHES

CyPress Publications proudly presents further adventures of Pete Grayson and his friends, as they find themselves embroiled in even more sinister, and potentially more deadly, events.

Available in early 2008

Here's a preview of *White Heat, White Ashes* . . . .

CHAPTER 1

I was awakened by the noise of the fire engines—heard the grinding of gears downshifting for the turn off Main Street, heard the pitch of the sirens drop as they sped north on the highway. I tried to fight the sense of panic sirens in the night always bring. For a brief moment I was eight years old again, and fire engines were converging on my house, while my father lay on the floor of his den in a pool of blood. I shivered under the covers, willing myself back to the present. I wondered if Mom was lying awake in her room, feeling the same cold sweat, the same fluttering in her chest.

It sounded like four or five separate engines, or maybe some were police cars—something big, for sure. I dragged myself out of bed and spread the slats on the blinds. I thought maybe, just maybe, I could spot a faint glow in the northern sky. Something orangey and flickery, not the steady yellow of the street lamps. I decided it was just my stupid imagination and threw my body back in bed, bouncing my head into the headboard.

Now I was really disgusted. No way was I going to get back to sleep again. The clock on my nightstand said 4:08. Four in the morning! Crazy time for a fire. It was a thought I was going to remember the next day, when rumors of tragedy spread through the hallways and into the classrooms of Bennington High.

The rumors themselves were like a firestorm, creating a draft that magnified their effect. Or so I thought. Being a world-class cynic, I was sure the story had been blown way, way out of proportion by the time I'd heard it. It was said two people had been trapped inside a burning farmhouse. Within minutes, the number of victims had become three and, tragically, only one had managed to get out of the building. The truth, in the form of a statement from a grim-faced Bennington Police spokesman, was even worse.

Jennifer and I watched the television on the little wheeled cart that had been installed in a corner of the school library. Principal Hyatt—despite his being totally out of synch with anyone under thirty, and though he hated like hell coming into actual contact with anything so gross as a student—had a few good ideas every once in a while. For instance, he was big on keeping us plugged into world affairs. Whenever there was what the TV people called "breaking news," several sets would be placed at strategic points around the campus and turned on so his flock could gather and become "part of an informed citizenry."

The policeman on the screen stood with a microphone shoved in his face by a young female reporter. Behind them was a smoldering heap of blackened timbers.

Jennifer gripped my hand and a surge of heat, unrelated to the scene in front of us, flushed through me. I squeezed back, then forced my attention back to the screen.

". . . and we just don't know yet. A neighbor says a family of six lived in the house, farm workers. We aren't certain, but think they were all in there—a mother, a father, four . . . children." The policeman choked up then and closed his eyes. The reporter started to say something but thought better of it. The cameraman, also recognizing the dramatic opportunity, panned in for a close-up of the officer's face. Tears could be clearly seen coursing down his leathered cheeks.

When he spoke again, his voice cracked. "We believe that . . . there is no evidence a single one of them, adult or child, managed to escape."

"Thank you, Officer Ferguson," the reporter said, as the camera moved back to reveal a third person, standing to her other side.

The reporter, oozing somber sincerity, spoke directly to the camera to tell viewers she also had with her Captain Frank Barnes of the County Fire Department.

She turned quickly and thrust the mic into the fireman's face. "What can you tell us, Captain Barnes, about the cause of this tragic blaze?"

The captain coughed a couple of times and rubbed his hand on his throat. He said, "Until we can enter the remains of the building for a detailed examination, it's too early to come to a definitive conclusion as to the origin of the fire."

"Isn't there evidence that this blaze was set deliberately, Captain?"

"There are certain suspicious items that must be checked, yes."

"I'm told," the reporter persisted, "that several gasoline cans can be seen around the periphery of the house. Are those the suspicious items you're referring to?"

"The presence of accelerant containers is always viewed with suspicion at the scene of a fire. But as I said, we can make no definitive conclusion at this time."

The reporter turned back to the camera, which zoomed in on her face. "So there you have it, live from the scene of a terrible tragedy which has occurred in this bucolic rural setting, just north of the town of Bennington, Texas, a normally quiet town, a town whose citizens awoke this morning to the harsh wail of sirens, and who have yet to understand the full extent of what has happened here."

With an exaggerated trilling of Rs, she signed off with, "This is Arrrrianna Lopez, Channel Three News."

Printed in the United States
202690BV00005B/94-99/A

9 780977 695874